JOSHY FINDS HIS VOICE

A story about speech and silence

by

Cynthia Pelman

Grosvenor House
Publishing Limited

The right of Cynthia Pelman to be identified as the author of this
work has been asserted by her in accordance with Section 78
of the Copyright, Designs and Patents Act 1988

The book cover picture is copyright to Cynthia Pelman

This book is published by
Grosvenor House Publishing Ltd
28-30 High Street, Guildford, Surrey, GU1 3EL.
www.grosvenorhousepublishing.co.uk

A CIP record for this book
is available from the British Library

ISBN 978-1-78148-242-1

Cover photograph by Cynthia Pelman
Front cover design by Topleftdesign.com www.topleftdesign.com
Title by Anne Freeman

INDEX

<u>DEDICATION</u>

For Omer and Tali.

With thanks to all the children, and their families, who have generously shared their stories with me.

Part 1: Silence

"We can make our minds so like still water that beings gather about us that they may see, it may be, their own images, and so live for a moment with a clearer, perhaps even with a fiercer life because of our quiet."

W.B. Yeats

CHAPTER 1

Nili

Joshy's eyes filled with tears when he saw me coming into the classroom. He tried to hide behind his teacher's long skirt. Claire, his mother, had already told me how he reacted to the previous speech therapist who took him out of the classroom to the therapy room: he screamed, kicked, and tried to run back to the class. He couldn't find his way back and ended up running into the library where some very surprised parents tut-tutted at the noise and commotion being caused by a rather small child and a very flustered teacher. We all knew that a very different approach was needed if Joshy was to agree to even sit down next to a speech therapist.

Having been forewarned, I decided not to take him out of the class at all, but rather to see if he would just sit down with me on the carpet and play, preferably with some toys which other children in the class would enjoy too, so that they would join in. Perhaps Joshy would enjoy playing, if not with other children, then at least alongside them. I hoped he would come to see me as someone harmless, or someone who is friendly, and not as a "speech-and-language-terrorist", which is what my partner Vito (who is only partly joking) calls speech and language therapists.

I carefully made no eye contact with Joshy, and concentrated on arranging my toy cars on the rug. Then I sat still, not saying anything. Nan, his teacher, understood immediately, and said, "Let's go and see those cars." Joshy approached gingerly, keeping his head well down and very carefully not looking at me. A few other children approached very quickly and soon all the cars had been appropriated, and Joshy remained standing on the edge of the rug, head down but eyes on the toys, clearly interested but not daring to push his way forward and take a car. His place, on the outside looking in, was already established.

* * *

After a while Nan called the children to come and sit at their tables to do some drawing. I sat on the side of the classroom watching Joshy to see what he would do. He seemed able to fit in perfectly with the classroom routine, drawing when the others drew, sitting down at the right time and in the right place and getting up with all the other children when they went out to play. But it was clear that he needed to look at the other children in order to know what he was being asked to do. During the hour I sat there he said not a single word. His head was usually down except for when he looked up briefly, eyes swivelling from side to side, to make sure he was doing what was expected of him.

In this way he managed to fit in perfectly, packing away the crayons, getting his coat off the peg and lining up at the door before going outside. To the untrained eye he was just a boy, no different from any other child in the classroom. His behaviour was exemplary, but he communicated with nobody.

Joshy's mother, Claire, was waiting for me outside the classroom, and after the session I took her to my room to give her some feedback about my first meeting with him. It was not easy telling Claire about this. I tried to make it clear that it was just the beginning, that with any child we have to take time to get to know them, to take it slowly, to feel our way so that we can make therapy feel like a safe place to be, but she seemed to be able to hear only the bad news: that it had not gone well and that Joshy had in some way failed again to be the kind of child we expected him to be.

* * *

Claire had already filled me in on Joshy's language: he knew the names of many things, especially cars and trucks, and loved making car noises. He was able to count up to four and enjoyed counting his cars – in fact he just seemed to love to count. He counted raisins before eating them, counted the cars in the school parking lot, and counted the family's shoes placed on the mat in the entrance hall. I had asked her to write down some examples of things he said at home, and she had written down, "one, two, three, four," "no more food," and "go park, scooter". When I asked Claire whether Joshy understood most of what was said at home, she initially thought that he understood a lot. But when I asked for examples, and she thought about it more carefully, she realised that when the family spoke to Joshy they would use lots of gestures and signs. They would gesture for him to come, or to wait, or to tell him they were going out. They would point at the dining table when asking him to come and eat. She started to realise that perhaps he was just good at watching people and picking up their non-verbal cues. Perhaps he didn't understand as much as she had thought.

Joshy was now four years and seven months old. His mother knew that other children of his age would have been talking freely for at least two years, using long sentences and chatting away with friends. She had looked up language norms on the internet and this confirmed her intuitive feeling that Joshy's language was very much delayed.

Claire told me she hoped that I would be able to help him to develop language so that he could have friends and talk to the children in his class. Claire looked down when she said this, but I could hear the cracks in her voice. But she also wanted to make it quite clear to me that at home he *did* talk, perhaps not like other children of his age, but he certainly talked. And the silent child seen at school was not the child she knew at home.

Joshy

Grown-ups are very big. They stand near you and their heads are high up, and you can see their knees. They talk very loud and there is lots of loud talk coming out of their mouth but you never know what they mean. Then they bend down and you can see in their eyes what they mean. They want you to do something. They want you to talk back. They fix you with their eyes, they talk and talk and noise comes out of their mouth. Their eyes get a funny look. But after a while they go away.

Sometimes they take you by the hand and want to take you to another place. They want you to go with them but you don't know who they are, they are not my mum or my dad, and I AM NOT GOING. That's when my tears come and I can hear screaming and there is a lot of noise and it gets worse and worse and louder and louder and in the end my mum comes and I feel better and we go home.

Claire

I knew when Nili said 'let's go and sit down and talk' that things had not gone well with Joshy's first session. I could predict what she was going to say. I had watched him at enough birthday parties, and sat through enough parent-teacher meetings to know: Joshy did not speak. Joshy did not participate.

Since starting nursery all his teachers had been giving me the same feedback: Joshy doesn't join in, Joshy doesn't play with the other children, Joshy doesn't talk. I found it hard to believe, as he always seemed so bouncy and sociable at home. Last year, after talking to me about it, one of his teachers invited me to look through the glass panel in the classroom door while the children were in class. Joshy was standing at the edge of a group of children, watching. He was holding on to a plastic dinosaur but not playing, not moving. Just watching. And not talking.

At home he would laugh, play, join in all our games and outdoor activities. But he didn't talk well. I knew what four-year olds can usually do, and our daughter Jenna, now seven, had been speaking with ease since she was one and a half.

I had managed Jenna's baby years easily, and I had read all the baby books while I was pregnant with Joshy, but nothing prepared me for the baby who Joshy was. The constant, ear-piercing screaming. Feeding him was a nightmare. He didn't latch on, he cried before, during and after the feeds. Strangely, he slept between feeds and it seemed that the only time he was okay was when I was not trying to hold him or feed him but when I put him in a darkened room, in his crib, wrapped up tightly in blankets.

Dealing with a newborn, constantly screaming baby did not come naturally or easily and I lost confidence in myself as a mother. I thought that I was not feeding him correctly, and after a while went to the doctor who said, "If he's putting on weight you don't have to worry about anything." When I went back a few weeks later to tell the doctor that Joshy was still screaming, and that we were getting no sleep, and burst into tears from exhaustion and worry, the doctor suggested that I had post-natal depression and offered some counselling sessions.

When I look back on those first three or four months I remember very few details. It felt like I was lost in an underground tunnel, where you were not allowed to sleep and your entire previous life had just disappeared into thin air. I lost my memory, and kept on forgetting to switch off the stove, or to brush my hair. I could barely take care of our daughter Jenna, then aged three. I seemed to lose any sense of who I was, other than an inefficient provider of milk. My breasts were sore, my stitches were agony and my mother was far away in England. There was no end to it. Day and night blended into one indistinguishable fog. I caught sight of myself in the mirror one day when I remembered I hadn't brushed my teeth for ages – and saw a grey-faced, frowning, oldish woman with matted hair and a demented look in her eyes.

I took Joshy to his three-month check-up. He had finally fallen asleep by the time I wheeled him into the clinic in his buggy – the buggy always calmed him down – but when I picked him up so that the nurse could weigh him he started screaming. She struggled to put him in the baby scale. He arched his back and his cries rose in pitch and volume until my ears were ringing. I burst into tears. The nurse patted my shoulder, and brought me a cup of tea. Then she sat down and started to write in her file. I tried to see what she was writing. Through my despair I was able to notice and to feel surprised about how I, in my former life a smart, sassy articulate lawyer, now didn't dare challenge her authority or even ask to know what she was writing. She wrote, Joshy howled, I sipped my tea and tried to hold it together so she wouldn't think I was an incompetent mother. Nothing I could do would calm him down and I just wanted to escape from that room and from her notes and her files and her judgements of me and my child.

At five months Joshy was still screaming at every nappy change, every time we went outside into the light, every time he was picked up from his buggy. Every little noise startled him. We couldn't take him out to the shopping mall – he would just scream and scream – so I stayed at home more, and Dave did all the shopping. It could not have been more different from our experience with Jenna. She was calm, she ate, she smiled, and accompanied us on shopping trips and even to restaurants. When she started school she quickly made friends, and everyone was charmed by her articulate conversation.

The nurse sent me off to a paediatrician to do 'further investigation'. More screaming, more notes. The paediatrician looked, prodded, measured, and said not a word – who could speak in the face of all that noise? In the end I said I would take a walk with Joshy in the buggy so that he might fall asleep, and the doctor told me to come back if he did sleep so that he could talk to me.

Talk to me? What was it he couldn't just write a prescription for? I went back to his room, Joshy finally now sleeping in the buggy, and sat down. The doctor paused and read his notes. Surely he knew what he had written only ten minutes ago? I held my breath. Here it came: the diagnosis. What-Was-Wrong-With-Joshy. And What-Was-Wrong-With-Claire who could not comfort her baby. At first I didn't know what he was talking about, and he did not think to stop and give me time to take it in. 'Neurological immaturity.' 'Sensory

Integration.' What did it all mean? More words, I couldn't follow him. What must we do? He referred me to an occupational therapist at a hospital.

When Dave got home from work I tried to explain to him what the paediatrician had said but couldn't remember the details. Dave had wanted to come with me to the appointment and I had said no. I was feeling so incompetent that I had to prove to myself I could do this on my own, that I could cope, but it was a stupid decision. Dave was sad, angry and then sad again. And we worried.

Chapter 2

Nili

It was my second session with Joshy. I came into the classroom while all the children were sitting down at tables, drawing. Joshy was sitting at his table with three other children, so I took a small chair and sat next to him, greeting the group with what I hoped was a calm, neutral 'hello' to everyone, not to Joshy specifically. I was trying not to make Joshy feel he was the focus of scrutiny. He looked up at me and quickly looked down. He had been drawing, or rather making endless looping circles on the page, and now he stopped and sat with his head bowed. My heart ached for him. He knew perfectly well why I was there and it looked as if he was hoping that if he waited it out, head down, he would be invisible and maybe I would just give up and go away.

I chatted to the other children and looked at their drawings, and then I took a piece of paper and started to draw. I was carefully not looking directly at Joshy but could see out of the corner of my eye that he was watching me. I started with a few looping circles, similar to those Joshy had drawn, and then made one of them into a car by adding wheels. I drew a few more shapeless circles and when I was sure that he was watching me,

I added a hat, two eyes and a mouth to one of the circles to make a funny face. This was a 'squiggle': something I had learned from reading Donald Winnicott and which had often stood me in good stead when I needed to make a connection with a child who was not speaking. I added pointy ears, eyes and whiskers to another of the circles to make an animal. I then silently offered Josh my felt-tip pen, still careful not to make eye contact with him and trying to show, through my body language, that I didn't mind if he didn't take the pen, but that it was his to use if he wanted to. He hesitated, looked at the pen, then looked down again and sat, unmoving.

I reached into my bag, pulled out a blue toy car, and took a blue crayon and drew a blue car. I put the toy car next to my drawing of the blue car. Then I pulled out a red car and put it in front of Joshy. He looked at it for a while, and picked it up. I drew a red car, still saying nothing. Joshy, without looking at me, put the red car next to my drawing of a red car. I pulled out a yellow car and waited to see what he would do. He picked up a yellow crayon and passed it to me, without looking at me. I drew a yellow car and he put his yellow car next to my yellow drawing.

I took a deep breath. Joshy and I had just had our first conversation.

I pulled out a cow. Joshy looked at me in surprise. What had happened to our game with the cars? "Oh! Silly me!" I said, with a grin. "I thought it was a car!" I put the cow back and pulled out another car. The corner of Joshy's mouth moved fractionally upwards- not quite a smile but a small step away from his usual worried expression.

Joshy had recognised my presence, and allowed me into his world.

* * *

Sitting at home that evening with Vito I tried to explain to him how it felt to be sitting with a silent child, somehow knowing that his silence was a place where he hid and felt safe, and knowing also that the worst thing, the thing most likely to make him retreat even further, would be to try to break into his silence. So how do I go about being a speech therapist, if talk is terrifying? How do you get someone to talk, if he prefers to be silent? And how dare you?

I knew Vito would understand what I was struggling to put into words. He is a man of few words. While I tend to talk in order to think more clearly, he thinks in order to talk. It was an old topic of discussion between us. When we first met, Vito and I often argued about how people understand language. I said that words don't have a definite meaning, because language only means whatever the people using it at the time, in a specific context, want it to mean, while Vito insisted that words had meaning, meanings which could be looked up in a dictionary, and that words were attached to their meaning. After a while we found out that we were both a little bit right.

For a man of few words, Vito had proved to be surprisingly gifted at puns. I am notoriously clumsy and forever knocking my elbows into doorways and hurting my funny-bone; Vito started calling my elbow an 'L-bone', the 'L' being the shape my arm makes when I have hit it once again and can't straighten it up for a few minutes. When I broke my leg and needed to walk with crutches, which I found to be almost impossible, he suggested we consult a "home*hop*athist". He jokes about buying semi-skilled milk and about his being self-unemployed since having left his paid job and gone into private practice.

But when I talked to him that evening about the fears I had about breaking into Joshy's silence, by daring to break into the walls which Joshy had built, Vito remained silent. Some questions don't have immediate answers, or maybe any answer at all.

Joshy

Grown-ups are big, but then they get down and put their face nearer you, right up against your eyes, so you can't get away. The sounds come out of their mouth and it is right next to your face and it feels like ice water in your face.

I know how ice water feels because my mum took me to swimming lessons and the teacher made us get in the water and it was cold and icy and it was wet and I couldn't breathe and there was a big noise in the pool, children shouting and the teacher's voice going boom, boom, boom on the water and I got ice water in my eyes and it was icy in my nose and icy in my ears and I can't breathe.

Today the lady came with the cars, little cars with doors that open. Last time all the children played with the cars and I wanted to play. This time the lady sat at my table and there was no noise, it was quiet and she had a blue jumper that was like the sky when my mum and dad and me went on holiday to that place where the sun made shadows on the floor and when I looked up at the big people the sky was blue, blue, blue behind their head.

The lady drew some car pictures and I played with the cars. There was a red car and a blue car and a yellow car. I opened the doors of the cars and I put the cars next to each other, in a line, so they were all together. I counted the cars. One, two, three.

Then she did some drawing, she did funny faces, she did cars. She got a cow. Funny. A cow not a car! The lady put the cars in her bag and said 'bye' and got up and she was big again, but when I looked at her she smiled and didn't say nothing.

Claire

I now know, having gone through this, that most mothers of children with language delay use the internet to look up how much talking children should be doing when they are two or three years old. We also sometimes need the internet to understand the incomprehensible jargon used by paediatricians and therapists. But at that stage, when I first started to realise that Joshy was not speaking,

I still did it furtively. I didn't want anyone to know; it felt like if I looked it up, and found something, that would make it true, and there really would be something wrong with him.

But at the same time I knew there *was* something wrong. The knowledge sat like a lead cannonball in my chest all day and all night. The weight of dread was immense. What if he never talked? Living in Cape Town, I found that there were few local organisations which could advise on this kind of problem, but there was lots of information being provided by organisations in the U.K.

I got hooked on the internet. The minute Joshy closed his eyes for a nap I was at the computer, reading Wikipaedia, Mumsnet, parents' blogs, and information put out by organisations like ICAN, AFASIC, and RALLI. I spent all my free time, sometimes late at night when everyone was asleep, reading about 'specific language disorder', 'expressive language disorder', 'receptive language disorder'. I read about 'overlap' – that a child may have more than one developmental delay. I read that children with language delay often have movement and coordination problems, or dyslexia, and some have autism. I caught myself switching off the computer in panic every few hours, then switching it on again and looking again. I couldn't look, and I couldn't stop looking.

When Joshy had his first birthday he gave us a present. He slept through the night. The occupational therapist had explained sensory integration disorder to us, and while Dave was sure, having read all the information which I was now sharing with him, that Joshy did not have this condition, I managed to get some tips from the occupational therapist, which seemed to help. Be careful not to expose Joshy to sudden changes of temperature, or sudden changes from dark to light, or loud noises. Try and see if there are certain fabrics that he doesn't like to wear, because they feel too scratchy. Cut off the labels, they may irritate his skin. Try to stay calm, even when Joshy screams. I already knew I had to stay calm because I thought if he could just have everything quiet and calm all around him, he would relax. I kept the blinds down and stopped listening to loud music, and the occupational therapist said those were good ideas. For once, I got it right.

Dave, seeing that I was not coping, had started coming home earlier from work to play with Joshy, and Joshy just loved it. Joshy sat up, then crawled, then walked, then ran, in his own special clumsy way, and delighted Dave by chasing after him in the garden and laughing out loud. They ran around and played ball. Dave taught him to ride a scooter, and Joshy's face said it all. He just glowed. I felt like the sad sack of the family – always worried, always dreading the next bit of information I would find on the internet, while everyone around me was having fun. But I was also overjoyed to see his growing confidence, to see his personality developing, to see him show his real self: loud, happy, boisterous and smiley.

As the weather warmed up, I got some sleep and got my memory back. My mother came from London to visit me and found a sparkling clean house with two charming smiling children and I was now managing to brush my hair as well as my teeth every day.

So gradually Joshy became calmer, started eating with us at the table, and to enjoy the food we were eating. He even started to enjoy going out with us to friends or to the park, although shopping malls were still off limits as they would set off his screaming fits, which threw me into despair and made me feel like we had gone all the way back to his early days.

But he did not talk. He seemed to understand what we said to him, and when we were going out and I asked him to get his shoes, he knew what to do, but I noticed that if I asked him to get his shoes when we were not going out he didn't know what I meant. I could see that it was probably the hustle and bustle of going out, with me picking up my bag, packing a water bottle and rice cakes, that gave him the clue that he should get his shoes. He really didn't seem to understand language at all.

My obsessive internet searching came back and hit hard. I was on the internet when nobody was around. I read about 'learning difficulty' and about 'language delay'. I found myself testing Joshy. I would point to the apples and say "Please bring me an apple", which of course he could do, and a little while later I would look out of the window and say, without looking at the apples or pointing at them, "Joshy, bring me an apple" and he would look anxiously at me, knowing I wanted something, but without any idea of what it was that I wanted him to do.

So I went back to the doctor, who looked at me searchingly, as if to check if I was still suffering from post-natal depression (I wasn't and hadn't) and booked Joshy in for a hearing test, even though I knew he could hear, as he would startle in his sleep at the slightest sound – a creaking floorboard, a key turning in the lock when Dave came in. The results of the hearing test were good, so now it was back to the doctor, this time to ask for a referral to speech therapy. I started to keep a notebook to try to keep track of all the professionals we had seen and all the things they told me and all the things I had read about and what the different diagnoses meant.

I also started to write down any words that Joshy did seem to really understand. But that list was a sad little list on an almost empty page.

CHAPTER 3

Nili

When I went into the classroom for our third session, Joshy looked up, and without being prompted by his teacher, stood up and came over to where I was sitting. He kept his head down and looked only at the bag with the toys, but at least he had, of his own will, approached me. Nan, his teacher, was watching and gave me a thumbs-up sign – we were thrilled. He seemed relaxed, as if he had known I was coming. I had told him, at the end of last week's session, that I would come again and would bring the cars again, but I didn't know if he had understood what I said. I also was not sure if he remembered what we had done in the previous week. For a small child, a week is a very long time. But one session a week was all the time I had at that stage, as my timetable was fully booked with all the other children I saw, in this school and in two others.

I had brought with me the same cars, as I felt he needed things to be stable and predictable, and I hoped that using the same toys would make our sessions feel more connected with each other, in spite of the gap of a week. I also brought some long strips of white cardboard, and showed him that we could stick the strips together end-to-end to make a road for the cars. I handed him the sellotape and let him take charge of that task. Then I took a black marker pen and made short lines down the middle of the road so that it looked like a road with two lanes. I spoke only enough to explain what I was doing. I handed him the marker and he took over that task too. He seemed happy to do this, and it was easy to understand how this was enjoyable – a task which was well within his capability, and didn't require him to understand or use language, or to look at me or interact with me.

I could just hear, amidst the din of the classroom, that Joshy was counting under his breath. He counted the number of pieces of cardboard, "one, two, three, four". He counted the cars. There were seven, and the way he counted them was "one, two, three, four," and then "one, two, three". He put the cars on the cardboard road and counted them again. "One, two, three, four. One, two, three". He seemed quite calm and relaxed.

I took out more cars. I counted them, but instead of counting as Joshy did, from one to four and then from one to three, I used all the numbers: "one, two, three, four, five, six, seven." Joshy looked at me and looked down, silent.

I held my breath. Had I overdone it by pushing him too fast, by showing him that there were more numbers than he was using? So I counted again, in his way: "One, two, three, four. One, two, three." I started to drive the toy cars on the cardboard road, and we drove cars back and forth, parking and driving. I started making car noises – vroom, vroom, vroom. Parp, parp! Joshy said nothing. I had to be really quiet as the teacher was trying to teach at the same time and I so wanted to say to Joshy, "Let's go outside and make a real noise with our cars." But our relationship was too new, too fragile, to take risks or make changes.

When the time was up and I had to leave, I explained it to Joshy, showing him my watch, pointing to the door, pointing to the cars, telling him that I would come back and we could play with cars some more. I asked, "Would you like that? Next time more cars?" And he looked right at me and nodded.

I saw his eyes for the first time. They were beautiful: huge, brown, with long eyelashes. He looked at me; I looked back. I smiled at him. He had worry lines on his forehead between his eyes. How could such a young child be so worried? I tried to imagine what it was like for Joshy. The world of school must feel like such a daunting and perplexing place. Perhaps he had no idea what the teacher wanted of him. Perhaps he wondered why his mum left him there every day and went away.

* * *

I remember my own mother telling me that my first days at school, when I was just five, had not gone well. I never went to nursery (too timid, too fragile, asthmatic, a poor eater) and started school aged five, never having been away from my mother for even half a day. That first year is not something I can actually remember in detail, but I do have a vague recollection of a time of bewilderment, and I have a photo of myself, the obligatory school photo, showing a tiny child with dishevelled hair, and a look of pure confusion in her wide open, staring eyes.

That feeling, of being bewildered, and of not fitting in with the rest of the world, is something I still experience occasionally. I felt it again on the evening on which Vito and I met. I had seen a poster advertising a free Tango lesson, and being at a point where life seemed a bit monotonous, I arranged to go with two girlfriends. But watching everyone else dancing, moving their wonderfully co-ordinated slim bodies, I felt that old feeling of being in the wrong place, in the wrong body, at the wrong time.

Joshy

The car lady came again today. We made a road and we drove the cars on the road. I put the cars in a line. All the cars driving on the road.

The car lady was making noises like a car and I liked that, I knew what her noises meant, they were car noises. I counted the cars, the lady counted the cars, one two three four. I counted the pieces of cardboard, one two three four.

Then she showed me her watch and I knew it meant we had to stop because that's what my mum does when I have to stop playing and go to school. So I was a bit sad but she said some words to me, she said cars, and something else, and I wanted to ask her when I could play again and she smiled at me, she was quiet, her mouth was moving and talking and I didn't know what it meant but it was quiet and nice so I nearly smiled at her.

I counted the children sitting at my table, one, two, three. At break I counted how many pieces of apple I got, one, two, three, and I counted how many biscuits I got. One.

Claire

When the speech therapist phoned me that evening to tell me that they had had a lovely session, and that Joshy had played nicely, I tried to be pleased. I mean, well, I *was* pleased, because it meant Joshy had agreed to sit with a person who was not his mum or his class teacher and had not been upset. But when Dave came home later and I told him, he said, "But what did she actually do? Will she teach him to speak?" And I realised she hadn't done much, just showed Joshy some cars, and he counted them, so what's the big deal? Of course he enjoyed it. He likes cars. And he likes counting.

Dave thought I should have asked her what she was planning and what she thought would happen and would he ever learn to speak. I knew I should have, but I didn't want to go through another meeting like the one with the previous speech therapist who made me feel like a bad mother because Joshy had screamed and kicked her and embarrassed her in front of parents in the school library. Some things are easier just left alone.

* * *

The thing was that Joshy was actually learning some language. I had gone on a sign language course for families of children with language delay, and this helped Joshy to understand what I was saying, and to use a sign to ask for things he wanted. The course trainers were lovely: they were kind and patient, and repeated the signs over and over until we could remember them. They showed us that you always sign and say the word at the same time, and explained that even though some people worry that signing will discourage their child from talking, in fact doing the signing and talking simultaneously actually helps the child to learn the words. All the mums there had children who were not speaking and for the first time I felt like I was not the only mother in the world whose child had this kind of problem.

So by the time Joshy started nursery he understood lots of words and signs, and could even say some words: school, banana (he said 'nana'), go-inna-car, fetch coat, and go-to-the-park (although that sounded more like 'go-a-park'). He loved going out for a walk in the buggy or to swing in the park, and that always calmed him down. He still hated anything which moved too quickly or rotated: the merry-go-round was off limits, the tyre swing which sometimes swung round and round instead of back and forth seemed to terrify him, but he loved swinging gently back and forth.

At the suggestion of the occupational therapist Dave bought an inflatable beach ball which he blew up only partially so it was quite squashy, and easy to hold on to, and Joshy found it easier to catch than a small hard ball like a tennis ball. He loved holding it, throwing it, kicking it. Gradually he was becoming a happier child, a child who was able to be comforted, who sometimes sat quietly with me when I read to him or sang songs and nursery rhymes. He seemed to be listening very intently, and he would rock gently to the rhythm, though he did not sing with me.

In spite of how well I thought things were going, my mum's second visit, when Joshy was two and a half, was tense. She hadn't realised that he was not talking and although she didn't say anything directly to me, I would overhear her when she was playing with Joshy in his room, repeating the same words over and over to him, trying to get him to talk.

She seemed to relax a bit when I told her about my notebook and that Joshy now had nineteen words. What I did not tell her was that I had read on the internet that a child of two and a half is expected to know how to say at least fifty words.

CHAPTER 4

Nili

I opened my bag to take out the cars, but Joshy had caught sight of an egg box which I kept in my bag. I took it out; he opened it and found the fake eggs. I had found these in a charity shop and loved the way they looked: really realistic, life size, perfectly smooth and oval, a pure porcelain white.

He took them all out and put them back in. Then he did it again. And again. I sat quietly waiting to see what this repetitive play meant for Joshy. He started counting under his breath. I made myself sit quietly and not intervene – remembering my supervisor from my student days who was always telling me not to talk so much in the therapy sessions. "You forget to listen. Give the child time to get his words in," she would repeat over and over.

The egg box had ten spaces, in two rows of five eggs each. Joshy was counting: "One, two, three, four." And again, "One, two, three, four." And then "One, two." It seemed as if he could not go past four, and had to go back to 'one' each time if he was counting more than four items. I filed this away in my mind as something important: was he struggling to remember more than four items of information at a time? This could mean that he had a memory difficulty, which would certainly make it hard for him to remember what new words sounded like. It could make it hard for him to understand sentences of more than four words. Or maybe he just liked counting that way?

Counting like this was what Claire had told me he loved to do, and it was what he had done last week with the pieces of card and the cars. Why this endless repetition? This was so different from the kind of play you would see with an average child in an average classroom. Joshy's play seemed to go nowhere, to be the same over and over. It seemed so important to him to keep on doing this. His concentration was total, he lost his habitual frown, and he seemed completely engrossed in his game of taking the eggs out, putting them back in the box and counting them. It felt like Joshy was creating for himself something predictable, something defined and organised by himself and not by the adults around him.

After a while, I thought I would try to join in Joshy's activity in some way. I didn't want to stop him doing what he was doing, but I wondered if he would let me join him. I took one egg and pretended to hide it up my sleeve, making sure that Joshy could see where I was putting it.

"Where's the egg? Where's it gone?" I said in an exaggeratedly funny and surprised voice.

Joshy looked up at me, visibly surprised, as if he had just realised that I was there. His face showed a ripple of changing expressions – was he irritated with me at breaking into his game? But then he reached out, pulled the egg out of my sleeve, and looked back at me again. No frown, and maybe the hint of a smile? It was difficult to be sure. He put the egg back in the box and looked at me again.

Then he took an egg and gave it to me, gesturing towards my sleeve. I put it up my sleeve; he took it out and put it in the box. So this was a game we could share.

The thing was, I didn't know how to explain this to Claire when I spoke to her on the phone that evening to tell her how the session had gone. My placing importance on Joshy's playing with me, on sharing a simple repetitive game, even though it was clearly important to him, now seemed so wishy-washy. Letting him count to four over and over was certainly not going to teach him more language. And yet somehow I had to show her what a big step Joshy had taken, in learning to trust me and to allow me to share his version of the world.

And trying to understand what counting meant to him could help me understand a whole lot of what it was like to be Joshy.

* * *

Joshy wanted to play with the cars, and he rummaged in my bag until he found them. I listened carefully, and he made a car noise, 'mmm, mmm' under his breath. I imitated his noise as if my car was saying the same as his. After a while, I made a new and different car noise. Beep!

Joshy imitated me. It was very quiet but he definitely did say 'beep'. His teacher was standing nearby and listening, and I caught her eye. It was a lovely moment because we both saw that Joshy really was able to have a kind of conversation, where one person talks and the other listens. It didn't matter that we were just making noises. The main thing was not so much about using words as it was about taking turns with another person.

So much of what I do in my work is inexplicable. I can't put into words how I knew when it was the right moment to push myself into Joshy's game, and how I knew what would be acceptable to him, or what would feel like an intrusion. At that moment, I was smiling, Joshy was sitting next to me, and we were playing. I sneaked a look at his face: he was not frowning. He was now prepared to have me near him. He seemed to trust me. I said very little in the session, and perhaps it was my very silence that made it possible for Joshy to look at me, to hand me an egg, and to break out of his silent isolation.

The noise level in an ordinary classroom is extraordinary. The normal joyful, excited and angry interactions of very young children are essentially very loud. The lawn mower outside, the frequent sirens of emergency vehicles going by, and the teacher's voice, all added to this mix to make it really difficult for an ageing speech therapist (we all start losing our hearing from age thirty: one of those bits of speech therapy knowledge I would rather not have) to hear the whispered sounds and perhaps words which I hoped that Joshy might say. I was desperate to get him out of the classroom to a quiet space. I had the feeling that the noisier the surroundings, the easier he found it to disappear into the noise and not to have to make any sound himself.

We need a quiet space in which to do our work.

* * *

Talking to Vito that evening about my day, we got onto the topic of how it is that anyone feels instinctively what the right thing to do is at any moment. Vito is a landscape restorer. He restores damaged sites after roads have been built through mountain passes, or land surfaces stripped in order to mine for kaolin. When a pipeline has been placed underground, carrying fuel from a port to an inland refinery, the long scar on the landscape needs to be smoothed and the plants carefully replaced.

Vito's current job was reclamation of a mountainside, which had been cut open in order to build a more level road through the mountain pass. He showed me photos of the site after the blasting. The devastation was enormous. The area adjacent to the site was still covered in local flora, the fynbos, but the area where the road had been cut through was blasted down to the bare rock.

Before the engineers went on site, Vito and his team had spent months identifying the plants which grew in that area, and removing those which could be easily uprooted without being damaged. This meant knowing which plants emerge in which season, as some disappear underground in the dry season and only emerge after the first rains. Some plants and seeds were currently waiting it out in special greenhouses, so that they could later be returned to the site.

The right plant at the right time. Vito and I are actually in the same line of work. Reclaiming damaged places, helping things to grow. Doing nothing when that is the right thing at the time, and being there with the right thought at the right time.

Joshy

The car lady brought a box with lots of eggs. I count the eggs: One, two, three, four. One, two, three, four. One, two. They are not real eggs because my mum doesn't let me play with real eggs and once I picked one up and held it tight and it broke in my hand and my hand was all yellow and sticky and I tried to wipe it off my hand and my shirt and my pants were yellow and sticky and pieces of the shell stuck on my shirt.

So I didn't want to touch the lady's eggs but she showed me that this is okay, she knocked one on the table and it didn't break so I knew they were toys and I could touch them.

The car lady smiles. The car lady talks quietly.

I took all the eggs out and put them back in the box, and counted one two three four, one two three four, one two. Then I took them out. Then I put them back and counted. It was so nice when they each went back into their special space and sat there.

The lady hid an egg in her sleeve but I knew where
to find it and took it and put it in the box. She's
a silly billy, you don't put eggs in your sleeve!

I put it back in the box, in its own place. The box
was full and nothing was gone, nothing was missing,
everything was okay, the same every time.

Claire

When I picked Joshy up from school he was in the
playground, playing on his own with one of his plastic
dinosaurs. When he heard me calling he looked up and
I caught a momentary glimpse of the frown, the worried
look, which he lost the moment he saw me.

In the car on the way home I asked, hopefully, using my
bright-and-happy voice, "Did you see Nili today?" Joshy
answered, "Eggs in a box, one, two, three, four." I didn't
know what he meant; surely they didn't use food in a
therapy session. But who cared? He looked so calm, so
matter of fact, somehow satisfied. I felt a tiny hope
growing that this time, therapy would work. Someone
had to believe in Joshy, someone had to give him his
chance, and maybe this speech therapist would be that
someone.

CHAPTER 5

Nili

In the school, at the end of a long corridor, there is a tiny, beautifully crafted space called the drama tent. It used to contain an old sofa and some lockers where the teachers could keep their handbags - an unused and wasted space in this school where every corner needs to be put to good use. It had recently been totally re-fashioned into a kind of stage. Made from an old four-poster double bed, donated by one of the parents, with the mattress removed and the legs cut down, it looks like a raised stage, and you can step up onto it easily.

Some of the teachers had donated saris in bright colours with silver embroidery, some long flowing scarves, and pieces of colourful fabric, and the school's art teacher had draped these over the four posts to make a roof and walls. Most importantly, the drapes can be pulled together like curtains in front of the stage.

I checked that it was not being used during the morning, and asked Joshy if he would like to go to the drama tent. He hesitated and looked at his teacher. She smiled and nodded, and Joshy nodded too. I gave him the eggs to carry, picked up my bag of toys and we left the classroom together. Nan gave me a thumbs-up sign. Joshy had agreed to leave the classroom.

I had spoken to the art teacher and she had arranged the space especially for us. There were flat pillows to sit on. She had wound strings of fairy lights around the posts and scattered tiny, opaque lights on the pillows in each corner. She had created a beautiful space of colour, light, shadow and secrecy.

We climbed into the tent and Joshy spent a long time re-arranging the scarves, placing the pillows and moving the lights around so that everything was to his satisfaction. It reminded me of what some birds do when they are preparing their nest before laying eggs. I saw the same kind of concentration when he was counting things – a total focus on organising his world so it felt right. We sat back in the quiet, gently-lit private space. Joshy took out the cars and the cardboard road and placed the road and the cars around the edges of the stage. He placed the eggs along the road. Then he counted the eggs and put them back in their box.

I sat in silence for a while and then I started to tell him a story. This was his story; I was simply putting into words what he was doing at that time, in that quiet secluded space. I hoped this would show him that it was possible for him to use his own words in that space too. I was telling the story, but it was not my story.

"Once upon a time there was a boy called Joshy. He sat in the drama tent. He put the cushions where they should be. He made a road. He put the cars on the road. He took out the eggs. He put them back in the box. He counted the eggs, one, two, three, four. The end."

Joshy sat, silent, not moving, looking at the toys. I waited. Silence. I could hear his breathing: deep and relaxed. This silence was not nothing. It was something.

I took out some paper and a pen and wrote the story down. I drew some cars and some eggs on the page, and read it again. Then I gave it to him. He folded it up, over and over, and put it in his pocket.

Then he started playing with the cars, very much on his own, but sitting next to me. This time he started making car noises: engines, sirens, crashes. I joined in by taking a car and making it drive on the cardboard road, making the same car noises he had made. Whatever he said, I repeated. I drove my car towards his car so that we met up on the road. Joshy smiled, looked at me, overtook my car and went on. We kept this up for a while. We played together until the end of the session. Joshy's voice was no longer a whisper, but a strong, loud voice.

Claire

When Joshy was two and a half, some old friends from London came to visit. We had been planning their visit to us in Cape Town for ages, and they had heard us enthusing about the beauty of this city for so long that they decided the time had come. Angela had been a friend of mine since we both trained at Law School in London, and after we got married the four of us would often spend time together. They had a child, a girl, who was now two years old and they thought she was old enough to take on a trip.

Our first few days were wonderful. We took them to all the tourist spots, which we still loved to visit, even though this was home for us and we had been there over and over: the wine estates, the beautiful beaches, Cape Point, Table Mountain, the penguin reserve at Boulders Beach. We had barbecues in the garden – one of the great pleasures of living in a warm climate when even in winter you get some beautifully sunny days. One afternoon, Angela and I were sitting in the garden chatting and she said, "I don't want to upset you, but aren't you worried about Joshy?"

I felt my heart beginning to thud. Of course I was worried, what did she think? But how awful to think she had noticed, and that she had probably been waiting for the right time to share her views with me. I knew it was silly of me, she meant well, but I felt... what I felt was humiliation. And then I felt stupid for feeling humiliated. And then got cross with Angela for making me feel stupid.

We had always been competitive with each other, vying for who got better marks on assignments, and here she was with her perfect two year old who was talking non-stop, while my Joshy, at two and a half, was not saying a word.

I brushed it off, saying something about his having been checked and he is fine, just a bit delayed. And that boys usually talk later than girls. I just didn't want to talk about it to anyone other than Dave, but at the same time

I was conscious that my not talking about it, my silence, was not so different from Joshy's silence. But I felt such a fierce need to protect Joshy from the outside world, where people did not understand him any more than he understood them. I felt that in some way only I could be the person to protect him in his silence.

* * *

In the spirit of including us in Joshy's therapy, Nili gave me a job to do: to keep a notebook handy and to jot down things that Joshy said at home. She had to give me lots of practice so that I would not write down what I thought he said, or what he meant to say, or what I thought he meant by what he said. I had to write it down verbatim, word for word, even if the sentences were incomplete and if sometimes I really didn't understand what he had said and could only guess.

Nili explained to me that because he didn't speak at school, and because he was so unsure about being spoken to, she could not assess his language through formal assessments. So instead I needed to collect what she called a 'language sample' which she could analyse. "A bit like a urine sample, only nicer!" she said with a smile.

This was new to me; speech therapy had never seemed like something to smile about.

But I just loved this idea of having a part to play in Joshy's therapy. Finally there was something real and useful that I could do to help Joshy to talk. And while it was a little discouraging in the beginning, when I had to write down his very short and broken sentences, I started to fill a page with words and phrases, and saw that the number of words he did actually know how to say was gradually increasing.

Joshy

I went to the drama tent with the car lady. It was quiet and dark and nobody was there. I closed the curtains. I had the eggs and I had the cars.

She gave me some more toys and I played with the toys. The dinner lady walked past the drama tent so I made sure the curtains were closed and I put my head down to wait till she was gone. Then she went away and I played some more.

I like that drama tent. I like the lights, lots of little lights, all over, up and down, and nobody can see us, and the colours are all around us and it is quiet. We had the cars and the eggs and a dinosaur and we played.

The lady told me my story. Then she wrote down my story on a paper.

Then we had to go back to the classroom so I put the story in my pocket. I folded it and then I folded it again and I did it again until it was very small so it would fit in my pocket.

I didn't want to go back to class until it was inside my pocket. My story is on a paper and I will take it home and show my mum and my dad.

CHAPTER 6

Nili

I sat in my office for a while before Joshy's next session, thinking. Claire was collecting a language sample for me, which would allow me to find out how many words and what kind of sentences Joshy was able to say now. But I still didn't know how much he could understand when people spoke to him. I needed both bits of information, the talking and the understanding, to decide what to do next.

I collected Joshy from his classroom and we went to the drama tent. I kept the eggs and cars in my bag and took out a little box with miniature toys inside: a chair and table from my dolls' house, a little car, a tiny fork, some plastic fruit, and a tiny teddy bear.

Joshy looked disappointed – I suppose he wanted to play with the eggs again. But I was very conscious of the fact that I only had one hour a week with him, and that there are only a few weeks in each school term, and I really needed to know how much he could understand. So I risked changing the context of silent play in our sessions and asked him if he could do something for me.

"Can you put the teddy on the chair?" "Put the fruit on the table." Joshy was able to do all of this. So he could understand sentences like this, with two main words, ('teddy' and 'car', or 'fruit' and 'table'.) This was enough to help him follow a short instruction.

Then I asked him to "Put the car on the table and give me the teddy" and I held my hand out to receive the teddy. He did this perfectly. I counted this as three main words (car, table, and teddy) and I didn't count 'give me', as that was expressed by my gesture.

But when I asked him to "put the fork on the table and the teddy on the car" he picked up the car, then hesitated, put it down and gave me the teddy. It was as if he had not heard the first part of what I had asked him to do. So it seemed that sentences with four main words (fork, table, teddy, car) were too much for him to process, and he could only follow the part of the instruction he had heard at the end: something about the car.

I could see Joshy was not keen to continue with this – his frown was deepening – so I packed the miniature toys back in their box.

I knew he wanted the eggs and the egg box, but I waited. I wanted to see what he would do to get them: would he gesture? Or would he just take them from my bag, where he knew they would be? Perhaps the idea of the egg disappearing up my sleeve last week, or its apparent absence this week, could spark the idea that there is a word for each thing in the world. If the thing is missing, a word can bring it back – or at least make the idea of what is missing more tangible.

Then Joshy said, in a very quiet voice, "Eggs? Get eggs?" I wanted to stay calm, not to over-react; after all, he spoke this much and more at home every day. But I was conscious of my taking a huge breath, and realised how I had been holding my breath from the first time I had met him. This was the first time he had spoken at school, other than counting to four in a whisper, and making some car noises. He had asked me for something. He had actually told me what he wanted.

Claire

When Nili phoned me to tell me the good news, the wonderful news – that Joshy had actually spoken at school – I had this fierce feeling of triumph. Yes! I knew he could do it! And it was not just counting: he had actually asked for something!

But then she told me about the test of under-standing which she had tried to carry out and some of my joy evaporated. She said that he could follow short instructions but not long ones, and that the kind of instructions teachers give in classrooms often have at least four main words – too many words for Joshy to process in one go.

Nili explained to me that if Joshy's teacher gave a very short instruction, so that he would have to do only one thing, like 'put away your books now' Joshy would know what he had to do. But if she said, 'put away your books and come and sit on the carpet', he would probably only be able to process the bit about sitting on the carpet and would not know to put away his books.

She also told me how much Joshy needed to rely on watching the other kids to know what to do. My heart ached for him. What must it be like to have to sit through a whole day of not knowing what to do?

I wanted to know at what age children normally start understanding sentences with four main words, and she told me it is roughly two words at age two, three at age three, and four at age four. My first thought, grasping at straws, was that Joshy is only four years old, so three words is not so far off the mark. But really, I knew, and I was not going to kid myself, he was at least a year behind all the other children in his class.

It's not that I was surprised to hear this from Nili. It was nothing new to us; Dave and I knew his language was delayed. It was just that hearing it in actual numbers made it so final, so clinical. It suddenly sounded so much more ominous than just knowing that he sometimes didn't understand everything people said. I thought, how strange that Joshy seemed to love numbers so much, but to hear his understanding of language expressed like that, in numbers – he can only do three, and four is too many – made numbers so very painful for me. It was so clinical, such hard evidence.

CHAPTER 7

Nili

I went to fetch Joshy from the classroom, hoping that he would again agree to come to the drama tent. I was a bit early for his session so I sat down in the classroom next to the dressing-up corner. Two boys were playing there, oblivious to my presence. They were wearing eye patches, and scarves wrapped around their heads, and were using wooden spoons as flags, having tied scarves to the ends of the spoons. "I'll be the captain." "OK, I'll make the sails." "No, I wanna do the sails, you make a flag." "OK."

What a world they were creating, filled with pirates and ships and flags, created with a few props but mostly with words and sentences. They were using their words to negotiate, to jostle for position, to make things happen in the way they wanted. They were using language to shape their friendships and to make their imagined world come to life in the real world. It made me think of Vivian Paley who shows us so beautifully in her books how children's 'play-talk' is actually their serious work.

All of this was what Joshy was missing out on. He did have some language, albeit a limited amount, and he used it at home. But here at school it was as if he entered a different world, one where his powers disappeared magically and left him with a silence which seemed to descend on him like a cloud.

His silence was separating him from the world of children and the world of social play. To 'have a voice' in the metaphorical sense is more than being able to produce sounds, and more than having words. It is having the kind of easy confidence in using language in order to make yourself seen and heard as a person. For a child of Joshy's age, using language should already be as automatic as driving is for me after all these years - something I use, with ease, to get where I want to go.

* * *

I use storytelling in speech therapy with most children, and over the years it has proved to be one of my most effective and rewarding tools. The language of stories has so much power – social and symbolic. I was hoping that by putting Joshy's play into the words of a story, I could lead him to a feeling that he could put his own stories into words. I wanted to model for him how stories get told, how they emerge out of our everyday experiences. Even with a very few words we can tell a story of what we are doing, and we can tell people what we are thinking when we are playing with our toys and using our imagination.

This time I had brought all the usual toys but also something different, a small but very scary-looking dinosaur. Joshy picked this up immediately and started hitting the dinosaur against the cars, against the puppets, the furniture and the eggs. He was making rather alarming crashing and whizzing noises. They made me think of fireworks, but also of sitting in a cinema where the surround sound is always too loud for my ageing ears, and where I feel assaulted by sound.

Was this the silent Joshy I had been seeing all these weeks? What did this sudden noise, so different from his usual silent self at school, mean? How was it that he was suddenly able, and willing, to make so much sound?

It was hard to know, and to risk making an interpretation which was incorrect would not only harm our growing trust in each other but would probably be verging on an incompetent and uninformed version of play therapy. So I started telling his story very tentatively, by simply describing what I had seen him doing.

"One day a dinosaur came. He was very scary. He crashed into the cars. He crashed into the table. He crashed into the eggs. He made a big noise."

I stopped there to see if Joshy would change something in the action being played out, or perhaps an idea would come to me of something else I could say.

Joshy looked at me. He crashed the dinosaur into the eggs again.

I resumed the story: "And then the dinosaur crashed into the eggs again."

Josh looked at me again. He made the dinosaur crash into the eggs, one at a time, four times. He made some crashing noises: "Wham! Wham!" Then he stopped, and seemed to be waiting.

So I said: "And then the dinosaur crashed into the eggs again, one, two, three, four. Wham! Wham! Wham! Wham! Four crashes!"

Joshy looked at me. He did not look away quickly in his usual manner, but held my gaze for a few precious seconds.

I took a piece of paper from my bag and wrote the story for him, using my biggest and neatest writing, and using very short sentences. I spoke aloud as I wrote each sentence. It didn't matter that he couldn't yet read; I wanted to give him something tangible to take away with him, in recognition of our shared story. I asked him if he wanted me to draw a dinosaur on the page with his story. He said "Joshy draw" (actually, what he said was "Doshy daw") and took the crayon from me and drew a looping shape with eyes and big teeth. A dinosaur.

So Joshy was indeed ready to talk to me, to ask for what he wanted and tell me what he wanted to do. I was struck by the paradox of it: he needed some measure of silence in order to speak. He needed to be in a place where his voice would not be drowned out by other voices, and where his thoughts could take their time to formulate themselves into words. This is what the drama tent gave to Joshy.

Claire

Nili phoned me to tell me that Joshy would be bringing home another story. She wanted me to ask him to show us the story and the dinosaur picture he had drawn, and for me to read the story to him. She explained that in this way she and I could both take part in his therapy sessions – Joshy would play at school, she would put it in words and then write down the story, and he would bring it to me and I would read it to him at home.

A kind of three-way conversation. Her idea was that it would show Joshy the power of language: that his ideas could not only be heard, but they could also travel from school to home if he wanted them to.

I read the story that evening to Dave, Jenna and Joshy. Joshy was beaming. Afterwards Dave and I sat quietly, thinking about what was happening. I was thinking how wonderful it was that Joshy was a person who was able to create a story. I thought about how his therapy had become a story in itself, with each session adding something to what was happening to him. Even in silence there are stories to tell, and stories to listen to.

CHAPTER 8

Nili

A week later we again sat secluded in the drama tent. Joshy spent some time arranging the bits of cloth so that the curtains were closed, and the lights arranged to his satisfaction, and then he looked at me. I sat quietly, knowing he wanted the toy box. I had added some other toys to the box: miniature furniture, small plastic animals and more dinosaurs. I wondered what he would do if I just sat there. He looked at me, his frown very noticeable, and in a very quiet, tentative voice, said, "Get cars?"

I smiled and opened the toy box and Joshy started to play. He arranged the cars in a line and counted them. Then he took out the miniature furniture and arranged it in a corner of the stage, as if designing a room. He put a dinosaur to bed, covered him with a blanket, and then suddenly the dinosaur leaped out of bed and crashed into the cars, knocking them over, and overturning all the toy furniture. "Pow! Wham!"

There was a real angry energy coming up from Joshy's little body. I quickly took out my notepad and wrote, talking as I wrote: "The dinosaur was sleeping. He got up and crashed the cars. He crashed the bed. He crashed the table. Pow! Wham!"

Joshy put the dinosaur back to bed and the whole scene started up again. The bed was knocked over, the blankets thrown to the side. I had been determined not to change Joshy's story and not to add anything that was not his, but the repetition of this violence got to me. So I said, "Oh dear, nowhere to sleep, the bed is knocked over." Joshy looked at me, picked up the pen and gave it to me. He wanted me to write. I wrote and spoke, "Oh, the bed is knocked over, nowhere to sleep."

Joshy said, "No sleep. No place for sleep."

I wrote it down. No sleep, no place for sleep. I didn't know what to think. I was so tempted to move the story forward, to understand why the dinosaur was having such a hard time. I wanted to connect the events with something else, a next step in the story, instead of the endless repetitions which Joshy was playing and re-playing. I held my breath, waiting, using all my self-control not to speak. Joshy said, "No sleep. No bed, no sleep."

I repeated his idea: "Oh dear, the dinosaur has no bed. No bed, no sleep."

Silence.

"Where will he sleep?" I asked.

"Nothing," said Joshy.

"Oh dear!" I said, "That's a bit sad, isn't it?"

My need for a good story had got the better of me. I just couldn't resist putting in my feelings about how sad it was that this dinosaur, who seemed to want to sleep, kept crashing into things.

But it seemed as if Joshy was alright with this; he pointed to the page to indicate that I should continue writing. And somehow it felt good, as if we had made this story together, just like any parent and child who chat together in the evening before bedtime and talk about what they have done in the park that day. This felt such a natural thing to do, and I remember interacting like this with my own children when they were little.

It seemed that Joshy could accept that his ideas could be put into language and kept safe by being written down. And I felt that he could also enjoy the fact that it was something we could share; we were sitting together and both taking part in making something with meaning.

* * *

At the same time, part of my mind was ticking off a bit of language which I now knew Joshy could use: the combining of 'no' with a noun ('no sleep', and 'no bed'.) These are important stages in a child's life: learning to express a negative idea, as well as learning to combine two words, such as 'more cake' or 'big car'. Between the ages of two and three most children start doing this.

I had asked Claire to write down exactly what Joshy was saying at home so that I could work out where he was in his language development. This would help me plan the therapy sessions, once he felt comfortable enough to talk in my presence, and to work on areas of language which he was still finding difficult. And now, while waiting for her to email me a list of two weeks' transcriptions, I was starting to hear his language in the drama tent.

Doing speech therapy always makes me feel as if two people inhabit my head; while one person is busy with the interaction, encouraging the sharing of feelings and thoughts with the child, the other is taking an inventory, making lists of vocabulary, word endings, and grammar, ticking off what the child knows and what I need to teach next.

Joshy was still playing, and this time when the dinosaur got out of bed to crash and destroy everything around him, Joshy said, "oh, the... oh, the bed break!" And he shook the bed violently.

"The bed break." A subject, a verb. A sentence.

Claire

The occupational therapist had suggested we teach Joshy to swim, as that might be a very good way to get him to build up his strength and balance skills, as well as to cope with changes in temperature and with noise. Our attempt at swimming lessons the previous year had been a disaster: Joshy cried, shivered, panicked, vomited and then refused to get into the water.

Swimming is a big deal in Cape Town. All children here learn to swim – it's a safety thing as most houses have a swimming pool, but it is also one of the main pastimes in a country where the sun shines most of the year. Dave thought he would try and introduce Joshy to the water in a fun way, without formal lessons, and that was a little better, but Joshy clung to him with an unyielding grip and would not let go. Still, after a few sessions in our own pool at home, Joshy started smiling and seemed to enjoy the water, while Dave was doing his best not to flinch when Joshy clung on to him with all four limbs, like a baby monkey holding on to her mother's back while she swings through the trees. Joshy held him hard enough to give Dave a bruise on his shoulder, and Dave does not bruise easily.

One very hot Sunday Dave put Joshy on a floating body-board in the pool, told him to hold on tight, and he walked around in the shallow end of the pool with Joshy lying on the board. The look on Joshy's face, when he suddenly relaxed and let go of the fearful clinging and just enjoyed the gentle rocking, was Dave's reward.

Joshy losing his fear of water was a huge breakthrough for the whole family. We had been dreaming of spending a holiday by the sea so that Dave could go back to his first love, surfing, which had been mostly put on hold since Joshy was born. So now we decided that in the coming half-term holiday we would go to Muizenberg, where Dave first learned to surf as a young boy.

For me, Muizenberg is walking for miles on the softest, whitest sand imaginable, picking up shells, and sitting on a deck chair in front of the colourful bathing boxes, eating chips and reading. For Joshy it had been, up to now, picking up shells at a safe distance from the waves, and sitting near me, playing silently and alone, counting his cars in the sand. For Dave and Jenna it was all about surfing. Now maybe we would be able to get Joshy into the water too.

Joshy

We went to the drama tent. I had the dinosaur and the bed and the table and the chair and the cars. The dinosaur broke the bed and he didn't have a bed to sleep in.

I gave the lady her pen so she would write it down and I folded it small to take home to tell mum and dad.

I wanted some pictures, I wanted a picture of a dinosaur and a bed on the page, but I didn't know how to ask the lady and then she said we had to go back to class.

CHAPTER 9

Nili

It was my ninth session with Joshy. That meant we had been working for nine weeks: a long time. Had I made any difference to his language? A lot had happened: he had agreed to come out of the classroom with me, and he had actually said a few words out loud and had asked me for what he wanted. These changes were not trivial, but if I was training a student therapist I knew what she would ask: did I have anything quantitative, anything measurable, to write in the notes after nine sessions? Something he could now say or understand, which he previously could not?

This was a difficult question for a speech therapist in private practice. On one hand I could see this boy and be in close touch with his family every week for as long as they were willing to continue, and this gave me the freedom to take a much broader, long term view than if I was constrained by working for the cash-strapped public services. On the other hand, this was costing his family a lot of money, and for Joshy's sake as well as for theirs I had to be absolutely sure it was money well spent.

I wanted my therapy to be different from teaching. I did not want to be teaching Joshy bits of language, the way we can teach geography or maths. I wanted our work together to be more like an apprenticeship: where I would make it possible, by showing Joshy how language works, and by mediating between him and the world of language, for him to start using more language, step by step, while I provided the support he needed at the time. The trick is to give just the right amount of support - not more and not less.

Speech therapists call this 'scaffolding.' In the same way as a builder puts up scaffolding for a potential building, which needs support in order for it to later stand on its own, I could create for Joshy a scaffold for language. There are lots of ways to do this. For example, I could start a sentence: "You like to play with...?" And he could finish the sentence: "Eggs!" and I could repeat the whole thing: "You like to play with eggs." In that way he would learn how to make a complete sentence, talking about things he liked.

I could scaffold in a slightly different way by expanding what he said: If he said, "Get cars" I could respond by expanding what he had said to create a more complete sentence: "You want to get some cars." Scaffolding is one of the basic tools we use in speech therapy.

The kind of scaffolding I was providing in the drama tent sessions was a bit different. I was trying to give Joshy the bare bones, the skeletal structure, of a story. Stories usually have a beginning, like 'one day' or 'once upon a time'; they have characters who do things and have things happen to them; the characters have feelings; the story gets resolved in the end by some problem being solved, and we mark the ending by saying 'The End.' This is a lot to demand of a child who is hardly speaking. But it gave me a way in, a model which I could keep in my mind when I watched him play, and a framework into which I could try to fit his developing language.

But even while I was providing a scaffold for storytelling, I did not want to interfere with his play in any way. What Joshy needed now was to be allowed to play in his own way, using his own ideas and creativity and imagination. So my story scaffold had to be limited to what I saw him doing, and to 'be his words'. I would speak his story for him, and model how it is for people when they have a thought and then put it into words.

* * *

I popped in to Joshy's class to give feedback to his teacher and to ask how he was doing in class. And what a surprise. Nan was upset; Joshy had had a tantrum in the classroom the previous day.

She was not sure what had set it off and she had been surprised as he was usually such a quiet, passive child. Claire had been told about it and at first I thought I would not get involved, as it was a matter between his teacher and his mother. But then I changed my mind; maybe I should try to find out what had happened. Children without language are often in some kind of trouble, usually due to a misunderstanding, and they often need someone to interpret what the teacher is saying, and to explain some of their behaviour to the teacher.

Nan's response worried me. Who if not Joshy had the right to be angry, when so many of his thoughts had to remain inside him, never shared with anyone, even with those who were making him angry? How much frustration can a person bear, when they have thoughts and can't express them?

There is a passage which I came across a long time ago, in a book by Viktor Frankl. I have typed it out and it is taped inside the front cover of my diary. What Frankl sees as the real and most important task of education is not to transmit information or knowledge like an object in a parcel, wrapped up and given to another person, but rather, "to refine that capacity which allows man to find unique meanings."

It meant that a large part of my job was to help Joshy find a way to show us what was already there, in his feelings and thoughts, so that if he wanted to express them, he would be able to. Even without words. And anger must be a part of that. And if he was having tantrums, we needed not to be upset but rather to find better ways to understand him and to show him that we understood him.

Claire

Joshy seemed to have gone from being the most silent child in the class to being in trouble for making too much noise! Nan called me over when I was picking him up to tell me how he had, 'out of the blue' torn up some test papers, kicked a teacher, and pushed over a chair.

It emerged that Nan had been called to a meeting, and a substitute teacher, who didn't know the children, had given them a task to draw something. She had asked Joshy to come up to the front of the class and tell everyone what he had drawn. Of course Joshy couldn't do this and perhaps he didn't know what he was being asked to do. So he had a tantrum and tore up the teacher's papers.

"It was just out of the blue," Nan kept saying. "We can't think what might have set it off and why he was so upset. We tried to talk to him but he just sobbed and I don't know if he understood us. I would like you to talk to him and tell him that this kind of behaviour is just unacceptable."

I have to admit I was furious. I am still furious. What right had the substitute teacher to put Joshy in a situation like that? I was proud of him for making his feelings known. I knew, from Jenna, how humiliated children often feel just because they are too small, too young to do things, too short to reach things. Jenna would sometimes get really angry when I wouldn't let her walk to her friend's house, which was just across the road, if I was too busy to go with her.

So what must Joshy have felt in the face of this very public humiliation by a teacher, if my competent daughter feels frustrated by the limitations placed on her just by virtue of being young and small?

After I finished being angry I just felt sad. I couldn't stop thinking about how it must feel for Joshy not to be able to tell people if he was sad or angry, or to feel humiliated and not have the words to defend himself.

I clung to the belief that Joshy would one day come out of his world of silence, and would be able to be, at school, the kind of person he was at home: smiling, engaged, and participating.

And I could now sense a change in him; he was starting to listen more; he made more of an effort to look at us when we spoke to him. Things were moving and changing, and if it took a tantrum for people out there to notice, so be it! Good for Joshy!

Joshy

The other teacher came and sat at our table and gave us papers. We had to draw. She said something and everybody knew what to do but I don't know what she said.

Then she said more and I still don't know. She said Joshua come here! And I went and she said tell us, and I didn't know what.

I felt something coming up in me, something hot, something wavy, I couldn't breathe, I picked up her paper and the chair fell over and I pulled her paper and it tore and I threw all the little pieces up in the air and we all saw them coming down slowly onto the table onto the floor.

I was breathing fast and breathing a lot and I went to the puzzle corner to sit there.

CHAPTER 10

Nili

The next week was the Spring half-term break, so I had to miss a session with Joshy. Time to tidy my toy cupboard, to send out invoices, and to go over the files of all the children I see, and maybe set some new targets for them.

I used some of the time off work to join Vito on a trip to his reclamation site. Having seen the photos of the site before the road works had begun, and then after the blasting was complete, I steeled myself for something quite harsh and shocking, although I knew Vito's team had now been working on the reclamation and planting for three months, and he was obviously pleased with how things were going. But he hadn't shown me any photographs of the process as it unfolded, as he wanted to surprise me.

It was a long drive through a beautiful part of the country, with wild flowers growing by the roadside, and green valleys lush with citrus orchards. As we approached the site Vito slowed down and pulled over to the side of the road.

The steeply sloping rock-face had made it a particularly difficult job as there was no soil to hold any new plants, and Vito's team had to make sure that there would be small pockets in the rock in which to place plants. They had tried to explain to the engineers that the last thing they wanted was a clean tidy slope. They needed random gaps and holes, with bits jutting out, places where you could put in some soil and position a plant. The engineers had been slow to understand and kept smoothing out the rock surface, but Vito's team kept guard, sometimes standing a bit too close to the blasting, asking for more potholes, more roughness. So in spite of the steep slope, the plants were now sitting securely in their pockets, looking tough and shiny and healthy. The denuded, scarred, bare rock face I had seen in the photos was now only just visible among the growth which was starting to cover the surface.

Plants need a safe place, just like Joshy.

* * *

I found myself thinking about Joshy during the break. He popped into my mind at the oddest times – at the checkout queue in the supermarket, at a restaurant with friends. I kept thinking how strange it was that so much had happened between me and Joshy in our nine sessions, but that most of it had not been about language, even though my task was to work on his language development.

It was that mysterious meeting between two people, when they impact on each other in the most intense way, but which often cannot be expressed in words, and maybe has nothing to do with language. And paradoxically, along with that impact, a transformation was occurring for Joshy: his words had started to emerge.

I kept revisiting our previous sessions. Was I reading too much into what seemed to be a turning point? Was what seemed like his new willingness to communicate with me, just a matter of his getting used to me? He had been speaking at home since he was three, so perhaps it was just that he was now more familiar with me.

But on the other hand his teacher had told me, on the last day of term, that Joshy had said to her, in a voice so quiet that she almost missed it, "We going Mui'berg". So he was starting to speak at school: not just in the drama tent, not just in our speech therapy sessions, but in the classroom.

It was such a pity that half term had to come now, just when things were starting to shift. I just hoped that Joshy could keep me in mind long enough for us to be able to start up where we left off.

* * *

I was looking forward to the coming school term. Now that Joshy was more confident in talking at school, I hoped to be able to introduce to him a more structured kind of speech therapy. With the language samples that Claire was now regularly emailing me, I could work out what level of spoken language Joshy had reached, and I would then be able to set specific linguistic targets for therapy. The part of me which needed an inventory of linguistic items to be ticked off was starting to feel less neglected. I made a list and checked how many weeks we had in the rest of the school year to make sure that I could plan his sessions effectively. I found myself counting: the next half term would be eleven weeks, then the long summer holiday six weeks, then the start of a new school year, with a first term of ten weeks... I was starting to count in groups, like Joshy did: eleven, six, ten.

Claire

Dave and I actually first met on Muizenberg beach. In those days, our teen years, the summer holidays were the time when my friends and I would spend long days baking in the sand, smeared with olive oil, which we believed gave us the best tan, and eyeing the boys. Few girls surfed in those days – it was mainly a boy thing. But we would go and stand at Surfers Corner, at the end of the beach, watching the surfers who were a breed apart, glamorous, tough, unattainable. Dave was one of them and on one glorious memorable day he asked me if I would look after his wallet while he surfed. But he was just too glamorous and I was too young and naïve for him, and we somehow lost touch, until years later when both our families had left South Africa and gone to the U.K., and we met again at a party in London, held by some recently arrived South Africans.

The memory of those days in Muizenberg stayed with us, and during our years in the U.K. we would dream about the day when we would go back to South Africa and back to Muizenberg. Muizenberg was one of the first places we went to see when we did go back, after Dave was offered a job here in Cape Town. Of course it had changed, the whole country had gone through terrible traumas and then the end of apartheid and a new reconstruction, but the sand and the surf were no different.

Dave had taught Jenna to surf and he was thrilled to see that there were now surfing schools for girls, who seemed to be starting as young as seven. I was hoping to just enjoy having time off from the school taxi routine, and take long walks barefoot on the beach, and sit on a deck chair under a beach umbrella (now we knew that baking for hours in the sun was not such a good idea) and read. But I took with me the exercise book in order to keep collecting Joshy's language sample.

This was harder than I thought – I never seemed to have the book with me when he said something particularly delightful, and when I did write down what he said, my heart would sink at the simplicity of it. Much of his talk was more like what you would expect of a two year old just starting to talk, than a strong and tall four and a half year old. Much like I felt when Nili gave me the statistics about his language level after the assessment, I was getting that sense of despair in my stomach that I hadn't felt now for weeks, just seeing, in black and white on the pages, how limited his language was.

It was also very hard to write down precisely what he had said. Nili had spent ages training me to write down his words, verbatim, mistakes and all. That meant that when he said "'mato" for tomato or "coppa" for helicopter I had to write down the errors, which seemed a bit unfair as I knew what he meant and so did everyone else when he said "'mato." Even at the local hamburger place they knew what he meant when he said "no 'mato."

The surprising thing was that as the days went by I had more and more words written down and when I started to count them I was amazed at how many words Joshy did already know how to say. Granted he was not joining them together. One of the things he said when he saw the surfboard we had rented for him was "Go. Water, in water, quick. Go." I would have thought this was quite a nice bit of talking, but now I knew that he needed to join those words together for it to be a real sentence, which even a three-year-old should be able to do.

So I read, and played with Joshy, and listened and wrote, and Dave started listening too and adding bits, and Jenna would come running over to tell me something Joshy had said, and – how wonderful! – even Joshy himself got involved, so that when he said something which he thought was cute, he would take my pen out of my bag and tell me, "Write!", and he would repeat it for me a few times and watch me to make sure I wrote it all down.

And as for the surfing – he was incredible. He suddenly seemed fearless: first practicing standing on the board out of the water, on the sand, rocking from side to side, but then going into the water with Dave, first sitting, then kneeling, and on one amazing day, actually standing on his board for a few seconds!

He spent hours belly surfing, first on smaller waves and then on bigger ones, getting more and more confident, louder and louder, and the joy in his eyes and in Dave's made me realise all over again the magic of this beach with its endless soft white sand, its warm water and soft waves, the place where I first set eyes on Dave and fell in love with him, and where Joshy found his own strong self.

Joshy

It is half-term. We in Muizenberg, I dig in the sand. The sand is white white white. The water is warm. Dad take me to Surfers Corner, he buy me black wetsuit. Daddy also got black wetsuit. Also a surfboard. Dad got his own surfboard. He like to surf.

Dad let me lie on the board, I hold on tight, and he walk next to me. He promise he won't let go the board. I feel the waves, they going under the surfboard.

Daddy say, come Joshy, let's surf!

So we go surf together. We go just one wave out. I lie on my board and Daddy lie on his board and we let go and we go! I surf lying down on a board. Next time I sit, I stand, I stand on the surfboard.

I can swim, I can surf!

Part 2: Talk

"Learning to speak is not the same as learning a new language."

Adam Phillips, The Beast in the Nursery.

CHAPTER 11

Nili

When I entered the classroom to fetch Joshy for our first session after the holiday, I was stunned to see how different he looked. He was tanned, and his new, very short and trendy haircut made him look older, more mature. But it was more than that. He seemed to walk with a spring in his step, and he seemed to have lost the hunched protective posture he had had when I first met him.

I had hoped that the break from school, and the active holiday at the beach would do him good, and it certainly had. His balance must have improved immensely, balancing on that unstable surfboard in fast-moving waves – and with the balance came improved posture and a more upright stance, which brought with it a new alertness, a willingness to make eye contact and talk face-to-face with other people.

It was wonderful to see how his body could help free up his thinking and emotions. I have seen this with other children I have worked with: the more upright a child is, the more he is able to alert himself to the conversation of others, and to take part in the conversation. I think it works both ways: Joshy's new posture would make him more able to listen to others, but would also make him seem more willing to take part in conversation, and I was sure children who saw him in this way would be more willing to make the effort to include him than if he were hunched over, making himself invisible. Body language is such a huge part of communication. And with Joshy's new confidence, he would hopefully be more likely to respond to a child who was trying to include him in a conversation or a game.

This was something which I wanted to see for myself and I decided to spend some time watching Joshy in the playground, as unobtrusively as possible, to see if my theory had any truth to it. And sure enough, Joshy was not hovering at the edge of the playground, watching the children from the corner of his eye, but standing with a small group of children looking at someone's new toy robot. I could not see if he was talking, but at least he was not alone.

Of course this was not the end of the story of Joshy's difficulties with language. Being able to play with other children would make a huge difference to his language learning as well as making him a more happy and sociable boy, but without specific and intentional language teaching a child with specific language disorder does not just pick up language the way other children do, as if through some magical powers in the air. Children like Joshy need carefully planned therapy, over many months and sometimes even years.

And while I was aware of the arguments about (and had occasionally been accused of) disrupting a child's creativity, or his natural development, by insisting on intervention through regular and frequent speech therapy, I also knew from years and years of doing this work that without this intervention, without that ongoing, intensive, specific and carefully thought-out mediation between the world of play and the world of language, Joshy would not pick up language the way other children do.

So now it was time to start doing some formal speech therapy, where I would set a language target and somehow show Joshy, through play and stories and games, how to understand as well as how to use that bit of language, and how to incorporate it into his conversations and into his stories.

***

I wanted to start with verbs, so that he would be able to make some sentences instead of using his preferred one-word or two-word communiqués. I also needed to do a lot of work on his understanding – not only of long sentences but also of some quite basic words like prepositions. He did not understand words like between, behind, under. He could not answer questions such as 'why,' which required him to give a reason for something, and to begin his answer with a word like 'because' or 'so that.' He was still struggling to understand words which express time: last week, the day before yesterday, the day after tomorrow, all seemed completely incomprehensible to him.

Claire

Nili and I met in her therapy room at the start of the new half term to discuss the plan for the term. I wanted to tell her about Joshy's surfing achievements and to show her the photos from the holiday. I was so proud of him, and we both had tears in our eyes when we looked at the photos.

Nili explained her therapy plan for the term: this term was mainly about doing 'real' language work, vocabulary and grammar, or, as she explained it to me, learning lots of words and joining them together to make sentences. Although Joshy already knew many words, (and in fact I was thrilled with the list I had compiled during the holiday), it turned out that things were not so great after all, because he was using many names of things, or nouns, but very few verbs. I knew, but hadn't thought of it in relation to Joshy's talk, that verbs make up the skeleton of a sentence, and that without a verb it is not a real sentence. So I was upset to realise that in spite of all the words he now knew, they were the wrong kind of words, or at least not enough of the right kind to make sentences.

I asked her how bad it was. Was he really that far behind other children, now that he was more willing to talk at school, and after we had had a wonderful holiday week, where everyone, including Joshy, seemed to be talking non-stop about the excitement of surfing and swimming?

She told me that he was about a year behind other children of his age, but in some areas even further behind.

She also wanted me to know that it was not only about talking: he still had quite severe problems with under-standing sentences which were long or complicated, and that this was making it hard for him to understand what his teacher was saying.

Nili explained that what he seemed to have was a condi-tion called Specific Language Impairment. Even though I had already read about this on the internet, I couldn't remember the details. She explained it to me: it is when a child fails to develop language as expected, for no reason that anyone can pinpoint. It doesn't seem to be due to any known causes, such as being deaf, or any other developmental problems. And just in case we thought we as parents were in any way at fault, or that we could have done anything to prevent it, she hastened to tell me that even speech therapists have children with S.L.I.

Nili explained to me that it usually affects both under-standing of language and talking. But because these chil-dren seem so ordinary, you wouldn't know a child has it until his teacher says something like, "I can't understand it, he is so bright, why can't he answer a simple question?" Or a parent may notice her child getting frustrated at not being able to say what he is trying to say. It is a hidden problem. And even though it is so common that some people think that there could be one child with S.L.I. in every classroom, many people, and even many teachers, have never heard of it.

Nili could see I was upset and wanted to show me just how much progress Joshy had made in his first term of therapy: he was now more willing to play with other children, he confidently came to therapy sessions and was relaxed and more talkative during the sessions. He even spoke in class sometimes. But she also explained that in order to learn language it is not enough just to hear it; you need also to use it. And because Joshy had for so long been silent at school, he had had very little experience of using the language he knew, of just talking every day, with other children.

I knew that we as a family made allowances for him, using gestures, guessing what he was trying to say, and somehow, as a joint effort, negotiating our way to understanding him and to helping him understand us. And I knew too that kids don't do that for other kids; if someone doesn't answer them, they tend to just give up and go and play with someone else.

But I left the meeting feeling really discouraged. How much therapy, how many months or even years, would it take for Joshy to be able to just be like other children?

But talking it over with Dave later, we started to see that what Nili was telling us was actually a very hopeful message: that now that Joshy seemed to have lost the fear of talking at school, and was seemingly more willing to take part in the talk around him, he would start getting the experience he needed, the experience of actually *using* his language in conversations, and we could therefore expect him to be making some very good progress this term. We use language to learn language, was what Nili was saying. And Joshy was certainly starting to use his language now, not just at home but at school too.

***

I know this is an old pattern of mine: when I am upset I just seem to shut down, and can't listen or take in anything. And only afterwards, mulling it over, do I start to make sense of what I have heard. It is something I had to work on really hard, in order to be good at my job as an attorney. You have to be able to keep thinking in the face of argument, discouragement, antagonism, conflict, or even just differing opinions. I thought I had dealt with that part of me, but here it was again.

And of course, applying that to Joshy, I could see how hard it must be for him to keep thinking in the face of an argument: I had at my disposal all the words in my famously expansive vocabulary with which to answer back, while Joshy only had a few words, and not enough of the ones he might need. So, looking to the future, I knew that it would be incredibly difficult for Joshy to put together the kind of essay I remember having to write in my later years at school, the kind of thing that asks you to give your opinion about an event in a book, or to give reasons for a character's actions.

And what I actually now knew, at the start of our second term of speech therapy, was that yes, Joshy had specific language disorder, and yes, it was quite a serious delay, and yes, it would possibly be very hard for him to learn letters and sounds. But even so, there had been really important and wonderful progress and we were set to see a term in which we could expect even more. And so, really, as long as Joshy was on an upward slope, and was happier at school, things were good.

* * *

This is Joshy's language sample which I collected during
that half term holiday:

<u>JOSHY'S LANGUAGE SAMPLE</u>
Half Term holiday October 2012
Age 4 years 10 months

<u>WORDS:</u>
<u>Nouns</u>: About 250 (I lost count)
<u>Verbs</u>: sit, stand, write, draw, swim, surf, pick
up, go, come, want (I wanna, don't wanna), eat,
drink, sleep, read, finish, take, gimme, stop, go,
tidy up, doing, kick
<u>Verbs he did not know or understand</u>: collect
(shells), sort (out), skip, prefer, improve, practice,
reverse, stretch, balance, be patient, try out,
disappear, bend knees, lean over, paddle
<u>Things he took literally:</u>
Take your time (Joshy looked around to see
what it is I wanted him to take)
I jumped out of my skin (Joshy thought something
happened to my skin when I said that)
<u>Describing words (adjectives)</u>:
big/small/little/quick.
Any extreme is "wow!
Sore.
Mungous (=humongous)
Yuk.
<u>Words for places (prepositions)</u>: there/here/at
school/on/in/far/near
<u>Does not know</u>: under, behind, next to, in the
middle, between, close, near.

SENTENCES AND PHRASES
Go now/go surf/daddy surf/Joshy me surf/
don't wanna burger/wanna surf/wanna more
ice-cream/big wave/no go home/shut up Jenna/
now now now!/More surf!
All the colours.
Daddy teach me more!
Shark come today?
What he doing?
Daddy kick ball.
Wanna go pizza.
More chocolate ice cream please.
Today little waves, no surf today.

Joshy

Nili draw some pictures: sit, stand, surf, fall off,
swim. All them things at Muizenberg.

Nili take me for a walk around the school. I look
at people doing stuff. All the children. Read,
write, paint, cut, rub out. Throw ball, catch, run,
fall. Lots of stuff to do at school. All them words.

I show Nili my photo album, here Joshy, me, me
surf.

Here surf with Daddy, Daddy stand on surfboard!

I can surf, I stand up.

Here my mum, she not surf, she sit. Mummy read,
mummy eat ice-cream.

CHAPTER 12

Nili

Claire asked if I would be able to take Joshy for two sessions each week instead of once a week, and I managed to juggle my timetable to do this. I had to liaise with Joshy's teacher so that he wouldn't be out of the class during important lessons, and we agreed that if he missed some of the free play sessions, or the Friday revision lessons, it would not be as bad as missing out when they were talking about new topics, or learning to count and add. I was really pleased that I could see him twice a week, as this meant that we would be able to work much more intensively, and based on Claire's language sample I had a long list of language targets to aim for.

Starting with verbs.

By expanding the range and number of verbs which he could understand and use, we could make it possible for Joshy to make sentences: a sentence by definition needs to have a verb. And in the list which Claire had sent me, I could see clearly how many words for things (nouns) Joshy had, but how few verbs he had in his vocabulary.

Many of the verbs I had chosen were words he did not yet even understand. So we worked for a few sessions using a picture book showing children doing various activities in the playground and in the classroom, and we talked about the things they were doing. I tried to use each new word many times, in different sentences, in different tones of voice, in different tenses, so that Joshy would get plenty of opportunity to hear the words modelled in sentences; this would not only give him the chance to hear the words many times (which he needed due to his really weak auditory memory) but also to hear how these words are used in real-life talking. "This boy is *jumping* over the rock. This girl *is jumping* in a puddle. *Jumping* in puddles is fun, isn't it? The dog *is jumping* over the rope! I wonder why he *jumped* over the rope? I wonder if you *could jump* over a rope. Should we try *to jump*? Wow! You *jumped* really high, right over the rope!"

I had introduced some other verbs the previous week by walking around the school and watching what the children were doing in their different lessons.

Then we started to work on adding '*ing*' to verbs, so that instead of saying 'Joshy surf' and 'Mummy eat ice cream' when showing me the photos of his holiday, he could say 'Joshy surf*ing*' or 'Mummy eat*ing*'. The next step would then be to learn to use the word 'is': 'Joshy *is* surfing'.

I used a small wooden block to represent the '*ing*' bit of the word and put out some picture cards of children doing different activities: hiding, falling, eating. I showed Joshy how we can talk about the pictures by saying what each child is doing: "This boy jump . . . *ing*." "This girl eat . . .*ing*."

He got the idea quickly and also got quite irritated with me helping him too much - modelling aloud too often what he now wanted to do on his own.

"*Myself!*" he said, putting his hand over the pictures and the block so I couldn't touch them.

And then, "*Myself!*" he said again, louder, holding up his hand and telling me to keep my distance.

Then he moved the picture book and the block to his side of the table, away from me, and started to go through them, one by one. "Jump-ing. Eat-ing. Walk-ing. Boy walk-ing. Boy jump-ing." He gave me a triumphant look out of the corner of his eye.

* * *

This discovery of 'myself' was not just another instance of his growing confidence in the use of language: rather it was what actually made it possible for him to use his language. His language was helping him to find himself, and finding himself urged him on in using more and more complex language.

Joshy was starting to become a person who could assert himself.

'Myself.'

It was one of those miracle moments which I sometimes have with children in therapy. I couldn't wait to get home and tell Vito about this breakthrough. We talked that evening over dinner about what it was that made today, of all days, the moment when Joshy was able to take charge, and insist on doing his own talking. I knew that part of it was that over time he had got to know and trust me, and that, just as he spoke at home with his family, so he could have felt that I was a familiar enough person for him to talk to.

But there had to be more to it than that: I was sure that it was his growing sense of his own power, as a swimmer, as a surfer, as a person who had his own story to tell.

* * *

In the next sessions, I decided to try to push things still further, and take his small sentences, 'boy falling', and adding something about *where* these things were happening: Boy falling *on* the ground, boy falling *out of* a tree.

Slowly, painstakingly, Joshy started making more complete sentences. We took out the holiday photos and looked at them once more. I remained silent and let Joshy talk. He paged through the album, commenting on each picture:

"Doshy surfing Mui'berg."

"Mummy reading book."

"Daddy surfing with Doshy."

"Mummy sitting."

Then I asked Joshy, pointing to one of the pictures, "Where is Mummy sitting?" And he was able to answer, "On a chair." I asked him, "Where is Daddy standing?" and he was able to answer "On surfboard." And I repeated for him, "Daddy is standing on a surfboard."

Words for places.

When he had gone through all the pictures we packed away the album and took out the cars. Joshy was now so much more comfortable playing and talking, and with only a little prompting was starting to be able to tell a story on his own. Instead of my having to tell the whole story by describing what he was doing, he now started to describe things for himself. I was now saying less and less, and leaving it up to him.

His stories had started to include not just characters and exciting events, but also sometimes a solution to a problem the characters had had: in other words, his stories were starting to resemble the structure of all classic narratives – fairy tales, Bible stories, myths and legends. This would stand him in very good stead when he would in later years have to write essays and reports at school – writing which usually requires a basic story structure.

I was still writing down Joshy's stories for each session, so that he could take them home and retell them to his family, and now he was also telling me what to write: he would play and talk for a while and then tell me "Write!" and would look at the exercise book to check what I had written, even though he could not yet read at all. He would ask me to read it back to him at the end of a session and sometimes would add in a bit more, if he thought I had missed out something important.

After I had written down the story, I would ask him something about his story. Was it a scary story? Did you like that story? Do you think Daddy will like that story? I wanted to show him that we can use language to reflect on things we have done, to evaluate our feelings about things. Language is not just for transmitting messages between people; it allows us to feel a sense of achievement, to look back with pride, and to look forward and to plan our future.

Claire

Joshy had had a few months of occupational therapy when he was three, and at the time the therapist said that he could do with a break from therapy, but that she would like to see him again when he was four. So we went to her for a review appointment.

And it was good news: She was really amazed by the change in him and discharged Joshy from her service. His balance was now good (of course! He's a surfer!) and his posture had changed too, something I had not noticed. She pointed out how he used to sit and even stand with his head down, as if avoiding people's eyes, but now he was making good eye contact, seemed much more alert, more able to understand her instructions, and when he did not understand what she asked him to do he said, "huh?" instead of just shutting down.

My car was being repaired, so we had to take a bus to the occupational therapist. There were no free seats, and Joshy and I stood in the aisle and tried not to fall over as the bus went over the many potholes, which are such a feature in our roads. "Like a big wave!" he said grinning. We stood in the way he had learned to stand on the surfboard, and imagined ourselves back there in Muizenberg, in the green water, standing, surfing and not falling.

"Big wave!" I said, as the bus rocked particularly roughly.

"Big wave," he agreed.

"Huge wave!" I said.

"'Mongous wave," he said.

Another bump, and the bus swayed ominously.

"Another humongous one," I said.

"Oh no! Another big huge 'mongous wave!" He laughed.

I wish Nili could have seen us, doing speech therapy in the bus.

What a change he had made in just a few months. It amazed me to see that the change in his ability to understand and use language was happening at the same time as his learning to swim, to surf, and to create stories with Nili.

Joshy

Nili take me to the drama tent and I play with the cars and the dinosaurs. This is my story, she write it down in my book.

One day, yellow car and red car driving. The yellow car driving, vrrm, vrrm. Red car driving, vrrm, vrrm.

Then suddenly dinosaur coming! A big dinosaur. Big scary dinosaur.

He crash yellow car. He crash red car. Yellow car say, Shoo! Go away dinosaur! Red car say, shoo! Go away dinosaur!

Then blue car come. He driving, vrrm, vrrm.

Big dinosaur come. He crash blue car. Blue car say, shoo! Shoo! And the dinosaur fall down. Down in a big hole.

I driving the blue car. You have to press button, you have to, you make it go.

Vrrrm!! No more dinosaur, cars all fixed now. Blue car chase him away.

CHAPTER 13

Nili

We were now well into the last term of the school year, and Joshy had been in therapy with me for four months. We had been working for quite a while on words for where things are in space: in, on, under, behind, next to. I used my miniature animals and furniture and talked about where each animal liked to hide away: the snake could hide *under* the cupboard because he was so long and thin, but the big elephant couldn't fit *under* the cupboard so he hid *behind* the cupboard. The little dog could fit *under* the bed so that is where he hid; the mouse was so tiny that he could fit anywhere. So he could choose to go *on top of* the cupboard, or even *next to* the little dog, *under* the bed.

Joshy enjoyed the game and found ever more inventive and funny places for the animals to hide, so I knew he understood what we were focusing on, but he still struggled to remember the words for 'under' and 'behind'. He knew that a special word was needed for a thing which went under something else, but seemed to be racking his brain and groping with his mouth to find the word. We went over and over it: I took out more and more animals and hid them under more and more objects;

we climbed over and under the furniture in the room and I let him hide under my raincoat, under the table, under the umbrella, while I pretended to search for him, saying "Is he under the table? Is the under the coat?" and Joshy would giggle and jump out at me.

But he just could not retain the memory of that word.

I decided to work on only one new 'place' word each week, and to take it all very slowly. I made a note to phone Claire and tell her that we would have a 'word of the week' and this week, it would be 'under'.

***

In spite of this ongoing difficulty with remembering new words, and with embedding the sounds of a new word in his mind, Joshy's stories were becoming more compli-cated, and started to include more varied events, instead of repeated crashes and repeatedly counting items.

I realised again how much I love working through stories and play, and not just using the traditional 'speech therapy' tools of objects or pictures to model or expand separate sentences. I much prefer to take a situation from the child's own real interests and his own active play and to use that to model the language as a story. I love how the play gives these children a context, a setting, where they can have their own ideas and then start to represent them in language, while someone is on hand to listen and encourage.

I had a good feeling about the many times I just sat there silently, listening to Joshy's stories. I was not talking and not modelling or expanding or doing anything technical or formal, but it felt like this was the essence of our relationship: I was a person who would not walk away if she didn't understand what he was saying, and would not correct him for saying things in the wrong way, but who would just listen. Being silent with a child in this way is not being passive. It is not doing nothing. It is listening, observing, waiting. It is being *with*.

Joshy's growing confidence was not just because he was more comfortable with me, but also because with me he was able to speak up and speak out, to tell his story instead of being a passive listener to the stories of others who could speak more than he could.

***

I was still thinking about Joshy's stories hours after my session with him. On the wall of our living room at home we have a photograph taken years ago by some anonymous photographer, of a Khoi-San tribe leader sitting in the middle of a circle, in a desert encampment, surrounded by the people of his tribe, of all ages, young and old, mothers with babies, and he is clearly telling them a story. Their faces show a rapt attention. All eyes are fixed on him. Nobody is doing anything other than listening to him, and the storyteller's face is animated, alive, his hands are waving around. I would love to know what story he was telling.

We all understand our lives through stories. Vito and I love to tell the story about how we met at that first Tango class I attended, all those years ago, in Muizenberg.

He was already a pretty accomplished dancer, and I was bored and looking for a new hobby. I had seen a poster on the wall of the Muizenberg railway station advertising a free Tango class at the restaurant at the top of the station building, and persuaded two girlfriends to come with me to try it out. The teacher at the class was doing some complex and stunning moves and everyone seemed already to know how to dance, and my friends and I stood against a wall reliving our teenage years when we were always watching other more popular girls and wishing we could find a way to become like them. A man came up to me and offered to show me some steps. I was nervous, clumsy, unable to hear what he was saying and feeling more than usually incompetent.

He stopped, stood still, and said to me, don't try to dance. Don't think about what you are doing. Just close your eyes and feel the music.

And out of that silence, that moment when I stopped talking and planning and evaluating and just listened, came our story. It happened at the one moment when I let go of my articulate, analysing self and instead just started to listen. I let go of all the words, the countless words in the endless essays I had written at school and at university, and just let the music take me away.

All them words, as Joshy would say.

Claire

Today Joshy brought home two stories, which Nili had written in his story book. I sat with Joshy and read each line to him, and we drew some pictures at the end of each line, so that he would be able to remember what each line was about, without having to actually read the words. Then he wanted to tell me the stories again. When Dave came home Joshy ran excitedly to him with the book.

"I read story! I read story!"

We were worried that Nili was writing down all Joshy's grammar mistakes and that instead of learning to use better language he would be stuck with his mistakes. I made a mental note to ask her about it, but in the meantime we were all so thrilled at this happy, talkative Joshy.

Then I started to worry about how many of his stories were about something scary or shocking – car crashes, robberies, shootings. I suppose that is the sad reality of life in South Africa, but somehow we had hoped that our children would not notice. Dave and I again decided to say nothing about it and to let Joshy tell the stories he wanted to – the last thing we wanted to do was to play the amateur psychologist and start analysing his stories. But I did wonder what Nili thought of the content of the stories. Was he unusually interested in violent stories? I made a second mental note to ask her about this.

The next evening, when I phoned my mum in the U.K. for our weekly chat, Joshy insisted on 'reading' his stories to her over the phone. When I spoke to her afterwards, I could hear she was crying. We were both crying.

I noticed, over the next few days, when Joshy told his stories again and again, how they were becoming longer with each telling. He was adding little bits in, not just extra sound effects, but also some more words. "We use language to learn language," Nili had said, and now I could see how it worked. The more Joshy spoke, the more his language improved.

Joshy

I got two story today.

My story number 1.

One night all the people sleeping. The car was parking. And then the man come. The man steal the car, he take it.

The family got no more car. They got to go in a bus.

The policeman come, nee naa, nee naa, nee naa. He look for the car but he not find it. No more car, got to buy new car.

Maybe the robber crash the car, CRASH!! Whooof!! No more car.

My story number 2.

The boy go to the beach, go surfing, he got surfboard.

Daddy driving the car, he put surfboard on top. Daddy park, he take surfboard off the car. Daddy and boy surfing, all the time surfing.

After surfing they come back to car. The window is broken. Maybe bad man break the window.

Got to get a new window, got to fix the window.

CHAPTER 14

Nili

I stopped by Joshy's classroom to ask Nan how things were going, and we arranged to chat during break. We made ourselves a cup of tea in the staff room and she told me that on one hand she was just thrilled by how much he was now participating in class, even putting his hand up once or twice to answer a question. He seemed generally so much happier, so much more part of the class.

But on the other hand she could tell that he sometimes just did not understand what she was saying when she was explaining something new. He didn't ever behave badly, or disrupt the class, but just sat there, frowning, looking at her with his big eyes, trying to understand what was going on.

***

In our therapy sessions we moved on to working on some 'little' words: those words which many beginning speakers, around two and three years old, still leave out: 'the', 'a', as well as the verb 'is'. The aim was to help Joshy to be able to say "Daddy is surfing" instead of just

"Daddy surfing" and to say "Mummy is reading a book" and not just "Mummy reading book".

Again I used small blocks of different colours and shapes to represent the little words, which are so short, and are spoken so quickly and quietly that you would hardly notice they exist. So it helps if you can see them. Joshy needed quite a lot of modelling and prompting, but was able to use these words in some of his practice sentences, although it would be a while before he could use them in his stories and conversation.

* * *

After work that evening, as the sun was going down, Vito and I were sitting on the balcony having a drink when we saw a guinea fowl on the grass verge across the road from our house. This is an extraordinarily comical bird, with eyes too big for his head, surrounded by sweeping dark eyelashes like an over-made-up courtesan. The male birds have ridiculous dangling turquoise and red wattles and a big, backward-curving yellow horn on their heads. Their white-on-black spotted feathers appear in paintings and pottery designs all over South Africa.

They roost at night in a tree near our house and their repetitive, raucous, unglamorous screech as they flock to their tree in the evening is in stark contrast to their glamorous eyelashes and beautiful feathers. The noise is something which, for me, is part of my attachment to Cape Town and which I remember from my childhood.

I took a photo of it to show Joshy, because I thought he might become interested in birds. Vito and I usually spend at least one day a week at one of the local wildlife sites, watching birds. It is something which has to be done in complete silence if you don't want to frighten the birds away – and I hoped that this would be an area where Joshy could find something to enjoy which was not related to school or to speech therapy, and which put no pressure on him to talk. A time where silence is a must, instead of a burden to be overcome.

* * *

I had talked a lot to Claire about vocabulary and grammar, but we also needed to talk about Joshy's speech sounds. Claire had told me, in our first meeting, how long it had taken him to learn sounds which even very young children could say, and how his speech not only started much later than any other child she had known, but when it did start, it sounded very babyish for a long time.

He did gradually learn more and more sounds, but a few remained at their earlier, younger stages: S, SH, CH and J. This meant that he could not say his own name properly, because his SH became T, and his J became D, so when he was younger, his would say his name as Dotty, not Joshy. Claire had helped Joshy to say SH, so now when he said his name it was 'Doshy.'

Instead of K, he was saying T, and instead of G, he said D. Their dog's name was Digger, which Joshy pronounced 'Didder.' Didder the doddie.

I explained to Claire that there was an expected developmental sequence for learning sounds, and that saying 'doddie' for 'doggie' was a natural and normal way to simplify what was a very difficult sound for many young children. When we talked about it last term I had told her it would need work, but not yet.

The thing was that during the previous school term I had not wanted to put too much emphasis on speech sounds: at that stage, my main aim was to help Joshy to lose his fear of speaking at school and to get him expressing his ideas and playing with language, no matter how faulty the grammar or the speech sounds. This term, however, things were different: Joshy had found his voice and his confidence, and now the time seemed right to work on the speech sounds as well as on words and grammar.

Sometimes things surprise you in this work. He had, all on his own, started to use the S sound correctly, and instead of saying 'tun' he could say 'sun'; instead of saying 'tum more' he could now say 'some more'. This is one of the knock-on benefits of getting a child to focus on listening to language: they start to listen to sounds as well as words and sentences. We usually played at least one listening game in our sessions, and I had shown his teacher, Nan, some listening games to play with the whole class.

So for example I would have a collection of small toys in a drawstring bag, and pulling out a toy seal, I would say, jokingly, "Is this a deal?" "Is this a meal?"

"No!" Joshy would giggle.

Eventually I would say, "Is this a seal?" and he would nod. I used lots of toys whose names started with the sounds Joshy was not yet able to say, and I saw that he could notice with ease when I was making a 'mistake' with my speech sounds and when I was saying a word correctly. So I hoped this listening work would now pay off in terms of his noticing the G and K sounds, and that he would come to notice that when I said "goose" and when he said "doose", it was not the same.

Joshy was also making an error in the word 'yellow', pronouncing the LL as D ('yeddow') and Claire had asked me if I could work on this with him, but I didn't think it was a priority target, as he did know the L sound and could use it in his other words, and this error with the word 'yellow' is a common one even among children with no language difficulty. This was very different from the problems with K and G, which were making his speech difficult to understand.

I tried various ways of showing him G and K. I used all the methods I knew and others which were suggested to me by speech therapy colleagues, but nothing worked. So I thought I would try a new word, something he perhaps had never heard, so it might seem to him that G was a brand new sound. Then he might realise that he had to do something totally different and novel with his tongue and his mouth, to create that new sound.

I showed him the photo of the guinea fowl and we looked at its funny wattles, its huge eyes, its lovely spotted feathers. And even though 'guinea fowl' is a long and difficult word, which I would normally never have used in teaching a child a new sound, I hoped it might just be sufficiently novel and unknown to him. We did some gargling to help him find the place where his tongue moved to the back of the throat. I showed him my toy crocodile who has a tongue in his mouth and who can lift the back of his tongue to make a G sound, and we tried out our new word.

"xxxxguinea fowl!!!!!"

And that was it. He found the place in his mouth and could say G. He did it over and over, enjoying the sound and his new ability. How surprising it was to see that a long word, which would be difficult for any small child to say, was the one in which Joshy's first G appeared! And how grateful I was to that ridiculous and beautiful bird. Next target: Didder the doddie.

Claire

I had eventually mentioned to Nili my concern about her writing down Joshy's incorrect grammar in the stories. She told me that she wanted to write the stories verbatim so that Joshy would not feel that he was being corrected while the storytelling was going on. Her main aim was to get him to express his ideas, no matter what kind of grammar he used. So she encouraged him to use sound effects, funny noises, and gestures, anything which would get him to feel comfortable being the talker and not limit himself to being the listener. However, in the actual language-learning parts of her therapy sessions she would be working on specific things in grammar, which he was not yet using, so that through modelling the correct language, in very carefully planned games which highlighted just that aspect of language, she could show Joshy the correct uses of words and word endings.

Joshy was still coming home after each session with his exercise book in which Nili was writing down all his stories. Some were illustrated by her and some had Joshy's drawings. There was always at least one drawing for each sentence so that he could 'read' each line. I also added to the book occasionally by downloading from the internet additional pictures to illustrate the stories, and this was a lovely way for me to get him to re-tell the story, as I asked him to help me choose the right pictures for any particular part of a story. He would then rush to Dave or to Jenna to show them and would tell the story again.

I could hear, and so could Dave, how with each telling the story became more fluent, how he needed to spend less time searching for a word, and how much longer each story became over the space of a few days. Now that we knew what to look out for, we could see that he was also using the new words and grammar that Nili was working on: little words like 'a' and 'the', and word endings like 'ing.'

As Joshy re-told the stories, he started to add more and more events, and asked me to write them down. We soon had pages stapled in, and pictures stuck on and folded down, as the stories became more and more elaborate. And in a wonderful process, which seemed to parallel the ever-expanding book, Joshy's grammar was becoming more and more correct at home, and he was using longer and longer sentences.

Joshy

One day, some houses burning.

The fire engine come quickly, nee naa, nee naa!

Oh no! The fire burning the fishies, the fire burning the dinosaur, the fire burning the car.

Oh no! all is burn. Dinosaur is sad. Now they need to find another house.

He splash water on the fire. He put out the fire. The water make noise, pshshshsh!

Then they going to new house. Then fire coming, fire engine coming, nee naa nee naa!

Water pshshshshsh! All on bed and cushion and carpet. All gone.

CHAPTER 15

Nili

We spent a whole session going over all the work we had done so far, the verbs, 'a' and 'the', and the words for place. I wanted to be sure that all of this new language was really embedded before moving on to something new. I was still worried about Joshy's difficulty in understanding long sentences, as I knew that even with the best will in the world, no class teacher can use only short sentences when teaching a class of children whose language is already at a much higher level.

So I thought a reasonable target now would be to help Joshy to understand and to produce longer sentences. I started by showing him how I could join short sentences to make longer ones. I started with the word 'and.' I took out our toy animals and some big cars, put a lion in a car, and then put an elephant in the car as well. Then, using a small wooden block to represent the word 'and' I pointed to the lion and said "lion", pointed to the block and said "and", pointed to the elephant and said "elephant." Then I said, "Lion *and* elephant in the car."

After showing him several examples, I asked Joshy to "put dinosaur *and* lion in the car," and "put giraffe *and* hippo in the truck."

And then: "Put lion and hippo and giraffe in the truck."
These were quite long sentences for Joshy to understand
and I could see he was at his most focused.

Once he could do this, I told him it was his turn to tell
me what to do. "Tell me two animals," I said, "Where
can I put two animals?"

"Lion in car," said Joshy. I put the lion in, and pointed
to the wooden block.

"Lion and.....?" I suggested.

"Lion and hippo," said Joshy.

"Oh!" I said. "Put lion *and* hippo in the car." Joshy
nodded.

"Tell me again, Joshy," I said.

"Put lion and hippo," he said.

"OK," I said, "lion *and* hippo in the car. Now tell me
what to do with horse and giraffe. You can say, 'Put
horse.....' and I pointed to the block for 'and'.

"And 'raffe.... in...in... inna car!" said Joshy triumphantly.
"Horse and 'raffe inna car."

"Good speaking Joshy! You said horse *and* giraffe!" I
put the two animals in the car as he had told me to do.

Then I made the task harder, by putting one animal in
a car and another animal in a truck: this meant that we

could have a sentence like, "Crocodile in the car *and* monkey in the truck." This meant using four main words: a big step for Joshy. But it was a step too far and I went back to the simpler sentences. This one would have to wait for a future session.

We took turns to tell each other what to do. One of us was the talker and the other was the listener, and then we reversed roles. I could see that Joshy was starting to manage to follow the longer instructions, to understand them, as well as to use the scaffolding I provided to be able to say these sentences.

* * *

We finished our grammar work and moved on to the storytelling part of the session. Joshy's story appeared at first glance to be about the fears all children have, or perhaps sharks featured because of some recent stories in the news about shark attacks on surfers. I didn't try to interpret his stories. My aim was still to provide him a context for using the language he had learned, a context which was not imposed on him but which came from his own imagination and interests. And today the thing that struck me in his story was that he was already joining a few sentences using 'and' to create long chains of events.

I often wonder if the repetitive grammar work I do in the first part of the session is just boring and perhaps even frustrating for children. But this felt like a pat on the back: speech therapy works!

Joshy was also being so much more active in telling me what objects he needed for his story and what he wanted me to write down or not to write down. This was a very different boy from the passive Joshy I had first met, who would wait for things to be given to him before he dared play with them. Now he was telling me, in a firm voice, what he needed. If I didn't have the toys he wanted for his story, he told me to draw a picture.

He was also now much more confident in talking aloud, and when people walked past the drama tent he ignored them completely and went on with his play and his story. A few months ago he would have drawn the curtains of the drama tent even tighter, fallen silent and sat motionless until they walked away.

* * *

In those storytelling sessions, the more Joshy talked, the more I held back and stayed silent. He needed me to be quiet, to make space for him to talk. It was the very opposite of all the modelling I was doing in the parts of our sessions where I was trying to teach him grammar, where I talked a lot more, and showed him how to use words and word endings. In our story sessions, I wanted not to push for language but rather to make myself still enough just to reflect his own thoughts back to him when I could see that he was not able to express them himself.

* * *

That night Vito and I went to our weekly Tango class, followed by an hour of free dance. Tango is a dance which does not have set sequences or steps and is largely improvised by the leader of the pair (usually but not always the male). The two dancers need somehow to communicate their intentions to each other without a word being exchanged. When it goes well (which is not that often, as I am still, after all those lessons, not very good at dancing and I still have really poor co-ordination) it is a wonderful, inexplicable non-verbal communication, something like what I felt when I sat with Joshy in the drama tent. I seemed to just know what he needed. Somehow being quiet, just observing and listening, and not talking, makes this kind of communication work.

As a couple I suppose Vito and I are rather quiet, even unsociable. I know some of my friends think it a bit strange that Vito can be in one part of the house and I can be in another and I am sometimes not even sure if he is at home. We can go for hours without talking at all, and then one of us will make two cups of tea and wordlessly bring it to the patio and we will sit there for a while watching birds. He will use his father's binoculars to scan the mountain for the two eagles which nested there last year. Sometimes we will watch the very long thin waterfalls carrying the day's rain down the mountain crevices to the streams at the bottom of the mountain. All in silence. It is a silence that is never flat or empty, but filled with shared thoughts, like the African sky that is studded with more stars than you could ever imagine seeing.

Claire

I was learning as much about speech therapy as any student in training. I had a lesson from Nili on 'scripts.'

She explained how children normally learn lots of language when their parents talk about what they have done that day, and go over all the events of the day or of an outing they have been on: "We went to the park today, didn't we? And do you remember, we saw the big slides? And you were very brave and went on the slide all by yourself. And what did Daddy say? He said, you are my big brave boy!"

So she wanted us, as a family, to go on outings, and to document our outings with photos and what she called artefacts: bus tickets, entry tickets to the aquarium, ice-cream wrappers, hiking trail maps – anything which was part of an outing or an activity we had done. Afterwards we could go over it with Joshy, talk about it, remember what happened, and model for him the kind of language needed for remembering and re-telling.

It's not that different from a story really, just that it would be about something real, something that had really happened, and that we all did together. We could use our language to plan our next outing, and talk in the future tense: 'We will go up Table Mountain in the cable car. First we will buy tickets, then we will get into the cable car, then we will go all the way up, and then we will be able to see, from that very high place, among the clouds, all the way across the bay, right across the water to Blouberg beach, and if we look to the left we can see Robben Island, where Mandela was in prison...' And later, when we got home, we would stick all the artefacts in the album and then talk in the past tense about our day, remembering where we had gone, what we had seen and done; using words for time like 'in the morning' or 'last week' or 'yesterday'.

All of this would give us a wonderful opportunity to use some very complicated language, and to use it over and over, until Joshy absorbed it.

So we started to plan outings: to the aquarium, to the penguin reserve, up Table Mountain, and we prepared a new story book called "What We Done" (Joshy's title – and I was *not* going to correct his grammar.)

* * *

Nili also gave us an exercise book for vocabulary, one of those huge scrapbooks. Each page would have words from a different topic. With Joshy's love of cars and transport, she chose the first page as the one for pictures of a fire engine, ambulance, police car, taxi, yellow car, blue car, sports car, jeep, trucks. My job was to tell Joshy what the topic was for that day, and then to take Joshy on walks and look for the different types of transport, and talk about them with him. Not just to name them, but to talk about what they do, what they look like, how fast they go, how they are different from each other.

The idea is to learn vocabulary in the groups or categories to which they naturally belong. I was already planning a range of topics and decided that the next topic would be 'clothes', as we had to stock up on summer clothing now that the winter was over.

I got the hang of it. We could join up the script work and the vocabulary work by finding as many words as we could, which we could then use in a script. So once we had a reasonable 'clothes' vocabulary, we could start a 'clothes' script. We could talk about going shopping for clothes, where we went, how we tried them on, how much they cost, and who bought what. Boys' clothes, girls' clothes, winter clothes, summer clothes, school clothes. I was starting to think in categories.

A funny thing I started to notice about Joshy was that even when he had learned a new word, and seemed to know it well, he sometimes just could not think of the word when he wanted to say it. For example, I bought kiwi fruit for the first time and the kids had a great time shuddering with revulsion while feeling the texture of the kiwi peel, followed by a look of amazement when I cut it in half and showed them the exquisite fruit inside, a pure watery green with a circular pattern of paler green stripes and black seeds in the centre. Joshy loved the look and the taste, and we talked about kiwi fruit then as well as later, and made a new vocabulary page for 'fruit'. Although Joshy was still struggling with the K sound, and said "tiwi" instead of kiwi, I knew now that that was not important at this stage. I just wanted him to learn lots of new words. We practiced the word while clapping our hands twice ('ki-wi': two syllables, and therefore two claps.) But the next day when we were at the shops he wanted me to buy another kiwi and he could remember 'kiwi' but he just could not think of the word 'fruit', a word which he had known for at least a year. I knew what he meant but I could see how frustrated he was, remembering that he had known the word the day before, had said it over and over, and was now not able to retrieve it.

Nili told me this is called 'word-finding difficulty' or 'word retrieval difficulty' and I was starting to understand that even though we were working hard on vocabulary, and even though his vocabulary was definitely expanding at an amazing rate, Joshy still continued to have this difficulty, with words being on the tip of his tongue but frustratingly not there when he needed them. I hated seeing the frown lines between his eyes coming back when this happened. My heart ached for him.

Joshy

My story got farm animals. Three cows, mummy cow, daddy cow, baby cow.

Here come a man, the policeman. He put daddy cow in river. Put baby cow in river, and put mummy cow in the river. All in the river.

I need two police. Nili give me more policeman, got two policeman.

Shark coming in the water, splash! Shshsh! Whoosh! Aaaargh!! And he eating them up. They all go bleeding on them.

And daddy cow coming and eat the shark up and the shark is all in his tummy now.

CHAPTER 16

Nili

The next weekend Vito and I went to visit the burial place of one of the very wealthy mining pioneers, Abe Bailey, who lived in the 1800's and is buried on the hillside above Muizenberg. The place was designed and built by Vito's father, many years ago.

Vito's father was killed in his plane during the Second World War, fighting with the Royal Air Force. He had had some flying experience, and gliding was a hobby of his, and in 1941, when the war seemed to be going badly for the Allied forces, he volunteered for the R.A.F. and went over from South Africa to England.

Vito was only two when they moved to England and he was not yet four when his father was killed. Vito and his mother came back to Cape Town after the war. He has only vague shadowy memories of his father, but he inherited from him a gift for understanding three-dimensional space and a creative, inventive way of thinking.

Vito likes to remember his father by visiting the Bailey grave site now and then. The road takes you along the side of a mountain covered with local flora, beautiful all year round. The site is halfway up the mountain. Across the road from the site, there is a cleft in a rock, which carries a seasonal waterfall. The burial site, a large, flat U-shaped platform paved with huge flagstones, is surrounded by a thick, low wall, which is in turn surrounded by protea bushes and aloes.

Bailey's headstone lies flat at the front part of the platform, at the furthest end of the U. The back walls have built-in benches also made of heavy stone, so that one can sit comfortably on them, facing the bay. Vito likes to sit on these benches where his father must have sat, watching the site being constructed.

The mountain slopes steeply down in front of the site. And what a view of the bay it gives. The blue sky of South Africa, and the darker blue of the water, with Seal Island quite far out on the left and the mountains of Somerset West and Stellenbosch on the distant horizon. During whale season it is the perfect place for whale spotting.

We sat there for a long time, not speaking. It is a space of grace, of a lasting and continuing beauty. It speaks of a long view, both across the bay and across time. Vito carries with him his father's binoculars and we take turns looking into the distant water for whales and sharks in the bay. We have sometimes toyed with the idea of buying a house closer to the sea, so we could walk to the beach, but I think Vito prefers this long view.

Claire

For a change, Jenna became the focus of worry, as she had been complaining of pains in her legs for a while, and recently it seemed to get much worse. We spent a lot of time having X-rays, waiting for the doctor, doing blood tests and worrying.

It brought home just how much of our time and concern had been directed towards Joshy and his problems and how Jenna, simply through being so cheerful and seemingly sailing through life with friends and at school, had lost out on our attention. I suppose that is a natural thing when one child has lots of problems but Dave and I felt bad, and made a conscious decision to try to equalise the attention from then on.

I mentioned this to Nili so she would know that I was not going to be doing so much speech therapy homework for a while as it just didn't seem fair to Jenna. I guess Nili was not thrilled to hear it, but we have to make our own decisions as parents, and it is always a matter of juggling the demands on a family and deciding what is more important at any given time.

Thankfully Jenna appeared to have nothing more than growing pains and the doctor suggested some physiotherapy sessions. We were so relieved – although I caught myself thinking: more therapy! But I quickly pulled myself together and booked a few sessions for Jenna. I took Joshy with us, knowing that it would be good for him to see that other people get therapy too.

And taking the long view, I now knew, and accepted, that Joshy would be needing therapy for much longer than Jenna's few sessions. S.L.I is a long-term problem and we would have to keep our focus on him for a long time. While not forgetting that Jenna needs us as much.

Joshy

My story today, I got lion, giraffe, tiger, turtle. Frog also.

Oh, they can't sleep, they need to sleep. And then come a turtle, and what did he say?

"I wanna sleep too!" And then is coming a frog, and he say "I wanna sleep too!"

Then the turtle come. Look, the froggie is not sleeping! And the gecko, and the turtle. They can't sleep.

They need to try! Try and try and try. Then they sleep.

CHAPTER 17

Claire

I had for so long wanted Joshy to be able to say 'yellow', not 'yeddow.' And even though Nili had said it was a small and not very important target at that stage, and that lots of kids say this word incorrectly, and that she wanted to work on K and G, I was determined. So we walked around the house and looked for anything yellow, and when we found something, I drew it on a huge piece of paper, put it up on the kitchen wall, and Joshy coloured the pictures in yellow. Good practice too for his hand-eye co-ordination (I learned something in all those occupational therapy sessions!)

The whole family got involved and we soon had lots of pictures on the page. We went into the garden and found a yellow flower, we saw a yellow car drive by, and we saw yellow wild birds with yellow wings eating berries in the trees.

Then I sat with Joshy in front of my dressing table mirror and showed him how I placed my tongue when I said 'yellow'. He struggled and could not come up with anything other than yeddow. I showed him the L sound on its own: la la la, lee lee lee. I showed him what my tongue did when I said L and he looked in the mirror and did the same; we bought ice lollies and ate them in front of the mirror, looking at our tongues when we licked the lollies. It wasn't that Joshy didn't know the L sound. He could say la-la, and little, and long, and light. But whenever he said 'yellow' it emerged as 'yeddow.'

We practiced saying 'hello' and I showed him how it was the same, that the second bit of 'hello' and the second bit of 'yellow' are the same: you say 'low'.

"He.....llo."

"Now say, Ye....low."

Nothing doing. Still "yeddow."

I was not giving up. I divided the word into two. He could say the first part, "Ye".

"Yeah yeah yeah!" we repeated, getting louder and sillier and doing high-fives.

Now say "low," I said.

"Like high and low?" Joshy asked, with the sideways glance and the half-smile he uses when he is particularly pleased with himself.

"Yes, just like high and low."

"Low. Low. Low. Ye.........................llow. Ye.......llow. Ye...llow. Yellow!"

There was no stopping him after that. He walked around the house: yellow shirt, yellow ball. We drove to the supermarket: yellow truck, yellow car. We bought fruit: yellow banana, yellow peach.

Nili

A few days later, Nan, Joshy's teacher, came up to me at break, really excited. Joshy had spoken in front of the whole class, in news time! He had told the class about his family's visit to the restaurant on top of Table Mountain. We could not get over the thrill of knowing he was confident enough to talk to the whole class. He had never participated in anything that involved talking to more than one person at a time. And although Nan noticed that his grammar was not what you would expect from a child of his age, the children seemed oblivious to this and were really listening to him, interested in what he had to say, clustering around him when he showed them the photographs his mother had taken, as well as the cable car tickets, and the souvenir pencil he had bought from the café at the top of the mountain.

* * *

In our therapy sessions, following on Joshy's success in joining sentences with 'and', I moved on to joining sentences with 'because'. This is a lot harder, because it involves thinking about a reason for something, and linking the event with the reason, and then putting all that into one long sentence.

I had some pictures to show Joshy. I showed him a picture of a boy standing in the rain. I asked him, "Why does he need an umbrella?"

"'Cause it raining," said Joshy.

I expanded his sentence, joining the two ideas: "Yes, he needs an umbrella *because* it's raining." I did the same thing with the next picture, of a boy getting into a car, modelling the answer to my questions.

"Why did he get into the car? He is getting into the car *because* he is going to school." Each time Joshy gave me half of the sentence (only the 'because' part) I expanded his sentence into a longer one, giving both the event and the cause. I was trying to model for him just what a long sentence would sound like.

I drew another boy standing in the rain. "What does he need?" I asked Joshy.

"'Brella," he said.

"Yes," I said, "he needs an umbrella because...?"

Joshy finished the sentence: "'Cause it raining."

I drew the umbrella in the boy's hand. "Now you say it, Joshy." I started the sentence for him, giving him a scaffold: "He needs..."

"He need 'brella cause it raining!" shouted Joshy triumphantly.

We grinned at each other. I drew a boy eating an ice-cream. "Why did he buy an ice-cream? He bought an ice-cream because..."

"It yummy," finished Joshy.

"You say it now, Joshy! He bought…"

"He get ice-cream 'cause it yummy!"

I drew a boy and a surfboard. "He is going to…?"

"He going Mui'berg 'cause he love surfing!" said Joshy with a grin.

I wanted him to know what an achievement it was, so I repeated his sentence and we counted the words. "He is going to Muizenberg because he loves surfing!" Nine words! Wow!! And even though Joshy had not said the words "is" or "to", or used the correct grammatical form of 'loves', I still wanted to give him credit for this very long sentence where he had combined two shorter sentences successfully, for the first time.

And as had happened before with Joshy, once he got the idea he just ran with it. He picked up all my pictures and put them down one by one on the table. "He go Mui'berg 'cause… 'cause he love surf!" "He buy ice-cream 'cause it yummy!"

We counted the words in each sentence and wrote down the 6's and the 7's in his book so he could show his family after school.

"All them words," he said, with quiet pride.

***

Learning to speak is not just about being able to say the words. It is as much about non-verbal hints and cues, as much about what is *not* said and what is joked about, as it is about words and sentences. And nowhere was this more noticeable than when Joshy was in the playground, trying to keep up with the games and the casual throw-away comments of the boys in his class.

The other boys were so quick. Things were only half-said and the others immediately understood and changed the game they were playing, or changed the rules of the game, or ran off to do something else, leaving Joshy bewildered, with his frown lines deepening. What had happened? He would run after them, hoping to find out.

Joshy found a friend at school – a child a year younger than him, who had recently come to Cape Town from Kenya. They met one day at break time. Lukhanyo knew very little English, so immediately Joshy felt comfortable, even competent, showing him around the school, explaining where he could play and showing him the hall. They became firm friends and Claire quickly arranged play dates so that Josh would have the experiences which his sister Jenna was having regularly – inviting someone over to play, to go to the movies with, to run and have fun with, someone who was not his dad or his mum.

***

We needed to carry on working on the G and the K sounds. I thought I would try a K, so I chose some pictures showing a few short and simple words, starting with K (or C): car, key, cow, kite, can (as in, 'I can surf!')

It was really tiring work for us both because even though Joshy could say the G in guinea fowl, and even though the position of his tongue had to be exactly the same for K as for G, he still struggled to get the back of his tongue in the correct place, and was more likely to produce a scratchy, gargling sound than a clean, pure K. He didn't enjoy it and neither did I.

I explained to him that it was a sound we needed because when children are little they use little people's sounds, but when they get older they learn to use older people's sounds. I knew how motivated Joshy could be once he got the idea that something was for big people – he had not only mastered surfing but on weekends took part in all kinds of difficult outdoor activities with his family, including cycling, hiking, and high-wire slides. But today we had to admit that it was not working.

I told him we would leave it for now and try again another time. "I know you can do it," I said, "but not today." He seemed content with that and gracefully accepted the reprieve. We decided to work on something different.

In the end we had a good laugh. I was trying to work on past tense verbs, and he was suddenly saying everything in the future tense. I was surprised and not a little upset – he had been making progress with past tense recently, and Claire's work with scripts had also helped, and I was quite hopeful that we were getting there. And then I caught sight of his expression – he was trying not to laugh. He was faking it! These were deliberate mistakes.

I picked up on his game and together we spent a good twenty minutes talking rubbish. I pointed to my nose and said this is my ear. He jumped up and down and said he was sleeping. I picked up a picture of a mouse and said this is an elephant.

We needed to laugh to defuse the tension of our hard work. But there was a lot more to it than that. It meant that Joshy had finally understood that language is just a code, an agreed-upon arrangement of how people communicate, and as such it could be changed, made into a joke, used in any way you wish when you want to be a bit funny and silly, as long as the other person knew what you were doing. It was, actually, a massive cognitive breakthrough for him. Knowing words is essential, but knowing how to make a joke is really using language to the full, really living. I could see in Joshy a growing ability to understand the ironies of life – and I knew what a lifesaver this can be when things get tough.

Joshy

One day, the fire engine say, I not want to drive. Red fire engine.

He got red wheels, he got a big ladder on roof. There was fire in a house. Daddy phone fire engine.

"Help! Fire! Come quick!"

The fire engine was cross. The fire engine not want to drive, but then the fire engine go quick.

He go because Daddy phone. Nee naa, nee naa, nee naa!!

The fireman take the hose and spray water on the fire.

Whoooooshsh! The fire was finish.

Daddy did say thank you to the fire engine.

"You welcome", say fire engine. "No more fire, I want to play. I be the driver, drive with daddy. I got fireman hat. Fire engine got new driver, me and daddy, we are driver. We go together.

CHAPTER 18

Claire

It was now high summer, nearly the end of the school year. The long summer holiday was a week away. I was looking at the language sample I had collected during our holiday at Muizenberg – was it really only two months ago? – and realised how much Joshy's language had changed since then. So I decided to collect another sample. I felt a bit sneaky, walking around with my note-book for a whole week and not being able to just relax with Joshy because I had to write down his sentences while I could still remember them, and this meant that sometimes I didn't answer him immediately when he spoke to me. He got a bit irritated until I showed him what I was doing and he seemed to be quite proud of the fact that mummy's paper was full of 'my talking'.

One of the things that was most noticeable in this new language sample was that he was talking in full sentences, not just single words or short phrases. It had happened gradually, and the person who pointed this out to me was my mum, because she was now actually having chats with Joshy over the phone, whereas previously she had been having those excrutiating one-sided conversations where the adult talks and asks questions, and the child says nothing more than 'uhuh'.

I had suggested to Joshy that he invite his new friend Lukhanyo to visit our house after school. I pretended to be folding laundry while they were playing in the kitchen, so that I could listen to what they were saying. I only felt a tiny bit guilty to be eavesdropping, and when I heard how much Joshy was talking to Lukanyo, and how they seemed to have found a real bond in their common interest in cars and trucks, I was really pleased I had made the effort to set up the play date, and that Joshy was enjoying having someone of his own age to talk to. They spent a lot of time swimming in our pool now that the weather was really warm. I lurked and listened and wrote.

Here are the sentences I collected that day:

JOSHY'S LANGUAGE SAMPLE
December 2012. Age 5 next week!

SENTENCES
I not want eat peas.
I take coat cause it raining.
We go drive in new car.
I got homework writing.
You give me that it mine!
Mummy Jenna take my car, not fair!
This the car I want, not want that one.
I cross cause she take my book.
I hate Jenna she a bad person!
I hiding under the table, you not see me!
Jenna hiding in kitchen.
I not have bath now, have bath later, I still busy drawing.

What we do after? After supper?
I was drawing.
Daddy was talk on phone.
I not want that one, I want bigger one.
First I finish Playstation, then I eat.
No, you take that car, I take the truck.
You want more cars? I got lots, I got trucks and cars and police car.
You got some more peaches? I like peaches, can I have more?
Come on, Lukhanyo, dive quick! You go first.

***

Even though Nili had asked me to write down sentences, I also decided to try once again to write down and count how many words Joshy knew. I found that an impossible task – there were so many. So instead, I carried on using Nili's suggestion for vocabulary, with a new page for each category of words. I thought it might be fun to do this as a family game. We chose 'places to visit' as our first one, and instead of using an exercise book (too much like school, and too much like speech therapy) I stuck a huge sheet of brown wrapping paper on the fridge door with magnets. I attached a black marker pen with string to the fridge door handle so that each time someone came up with a new idea they could add it to the list – either writing the word or drawing a picture.

Joshy's vocabulary was growing, but what was also lovely to see was that even though he still struggled to learn a new word, and needed Jenna or me to repeat it to him over and over, and to help him practice saying the new words, he had a steely determination to master every word on our sheets. I ran out of ideas for categories and Nili suggested we find categories which included verbs, so we added a sheet for 'things we do in the park', 'our favourite sports and how we do them', 'things you can do with your hands' (write, cut, throw a ball, draw, slice, mix, switch on...) and 'things you do when you are surfing' (balance, stand, wait, watch out for sharks!)

Nili

Claire had sent me an SMS to tell me that Joshy could now say 'yellow'. I just loved the way she took things on, her resolute belief that he would be able to do things that other people might have said he was not ready for. It was more than teaching him to say yellow – it extended to the surfing, and to the kind of things they did over the weekends: obstacle courses, bike rides, and learning new crafts. One Saturday they had gone, as a family, on a course to learn how to decorate tabletops with mosaic. And in Joshy I could see the same motivation to master things which were difficult or new.

I wanted to hear the 'yellow' for myself so drew a fire engine and asked him if he would like to colour it in, and when he said yes, I handed him a yellow crayon.

"No! Fire engine is red!" he said.

I joked with him: "Oh, I thought a fire engine is this colour."

"No! Not yellow! Red!" said Joshy. And then he gave a little smile, and repeated, as if to himself, "Yellow. Yellow."

* * *

We did some more work on telling stories in the past tense. Joshy was certainly able to understand the difference between things that are happening now and things that happened in the past. But although Joshy was starting to get the use of 'was' ('he was happy', 'he was sad') he was still struggling with the -ed endings.

'Jump' becomes 'jumped', and the 'ed' at the end of the word is pronounced not as it is written, with a D, but as a very quiet T. It would be very hard for a child with Joshy's difficulties to even notice that quiet T, let alone join it onto the word 'jump.'

And to make things even harder, there are all the exception forms in English grammar: go becomes went, eat becomes ate, sleep becomes slept. This was even harder for him than adding 'ed', as it meant learning a whole new word each time, and new words were really difficult for Joshy with his very poor auditory memory skills.

We also needed to carry on working on words for time, such as this week, last week, next week. The day after tomorrow. The day before yesterday.

Words for time are so complex, so difficult to explain. Time past was simply gone, and how could I be sure he understood that I meant the trip he took last week, and not the one they did two weeks ago? He was getting very confused, saying things like 'last yesterday' (by which, I found out, he meant the day before yesterday.)

We started using a calendar, and with Claire's help we drew a tiny picture in each square for each day, showing something Joshy had done on that day. So at the end of each week we could go over the previous pages and talk about how on Monday he went swimming, but last week he didn't swim because it was raining. The week before last, it didn't rain.

I could see his frown returning. It was all so abstract, so hard to remember. Once again, I decided to leave it for now and to return to it at a later session. We did some listening work with words starting with K and I asked him to put a sticker on a sheet of paper every time he heard a word starting with K. He did this really well and I didn't want to spoil his good mood by asking him to try to say the sound again so I put that off for another session too.

* * *

Oh dear. Perhaps I was treading too carefully? Perhaps I needed to be just a little more assertive with the children, and try to move on a little more quickly. Who can judge the right pace for this kind of work? Speech therapists often meet up with each other for peer supervision, and we attend many training days to keep up with new research, but we seldom have the time or opportunity to actually watch each other at work. And in spite of all our technical knowledge about linguistics and about how children develop or don't develop language, there is an aspect of therapy which remains a mysterious process – neither science nor teaching. What do other therapists actually *do* in therapy? And how do they know when to do it and how to do it?

In spite of all his progress, there was no denying that Joshy was still struggling to make longer sentences and still could not always understand what Nan was saying in the classroom. He made errors with long words, like saying 'nana' for banana, and 'puter' for computer. He said 'aminal' for animal and 'hetopter' for helicopter. And his word-finding difficulties were still apparent. Sometimes he just could not think of a word which he had used and understood only a day or so earlier. But on the other hand he was so motivated. In spite of all the hard work he had to do on a daily basis, just keeping up with the class, he did not give up.

Joshy

One day there was a dinosaur. He was little.
He want to be a big dinosaur.

Can he get bigger? Make him be bigger?
I think, I say abracadabra and make him bigger.

ABRACADABRA!!
Oh! Not bigger, still tiny. He was still tiny.

I give him a crown on his head, and I say abracadabra.

ABRACADABRA!
Oh! he still tiny!

We get a magic wand.

ABRACADABRA!
Oh! He was still tiny.

Maybe if he eat lot of apples, he will get big.

But he can't open his mouth. So he can't eat.

Nili draw a glass of water for dinosaur to drink.
He drink it all up! Slurp! And still he not bigger!

We need to say it very loud.

ABRACADABRA!!

And he still was tiny.

What we going to do?

The end.

Part 3: Joshy

"Solitude is fine but you need someone to tell that solitude is fine."

Honoré de Balzac

Chapter 19

Nili

Joshy was now five and a new school year had started. He was now in the Reception class, which meant that he had a new teacher, Yasmine, who had not experienced his early struggles or his successes of the past year. She would have read Nan's reports from the previous year but would not really know how Joshy's S.L.I. had affected his ability to learn, or his behaviour in the classroom. Claire was really concerned, and she and I talked on the phone about how to make the handover as seamless as possible for Joshy.

Although Yasmine was known to be a very good teacher, we were both anxious. Claire was particularly worried that Yasmine would think Joshy was lazy, or stupid. I was worried that she would think he was simply being rude or wilful if he looked away when she spoke to him, or if he didn't carry out the instructions she gave. And we were both worried about his ability to learn letters and sounds, and start reading, which was the main target for this Reception year. Some schools start reading later, at age six, but this school prided itself on its ability to get children reading, or at least ready for reading, before the age of six. There was a lot of controversy about this, and to be honest I wished that Joshy was at a different school where he would still have a whole year to consolidate his language before starting to read.

I knew, from meeting the same issues with other children with S.L.I. with whom I had previously worked, that most teachers don't have any training in language delay. In my conversations with friends, family, and teachers, the way people understood the idea of 'language difficulty' was in relation to struggling to learn English when your family spoke another language. In South Africa, with our new democracy, which now aimed to offer an equal quality of schooling to all children, there was a new awareness about the multiplicity of languages being spoken in the country, and a strong feeling that a child had the right to be educated in his home language. And with at least thirteen official languages being spoken around the country, the reality was that most schools taught in English, and that most children had to learn to read and write English, whether or not they spoke it at home. This meant that many children in South Africa have 'language difficulty'. But only a few have S.L.I.

Well, not so few. In fact, as I had told Claire frequently, it is said that there may be one in every classroom. That makes thousands.

The thing is that few people know what S.L.I. is. There have been a few popular movies and books recently about famous people who stutter, or about autism, as well as some personal accounts in the press of successful local businessmen who talk about their dyslexia, so generally people seem to be much more aware of language problems than they were ten or twenty years ago.

But when I try to explain that children like Joshy are not deaf, do not stutter, and do not have autism, and can actually be as bright as any child you could meet, I can never seem to get people to understand what the problem is.

It is a kind of hidden disability; unless you are trained to see it, or you are a parent of a child with S.L.I., you wouldn't know if a child has it.

Claire, Dave and I had tried to set up a meeting with the new teacher before the end of the school year but it didn't work out. However we did manage a meeting with the school principal and Joshy's teacher, Nan, and in that meeting an idea emerged.

Nan said that it had taken her, a very experienced teacher, at least three months of watching me work, getting feedback from me and from Claire, and seeing the changes in Joshy himself, to understand what S.L.I was. "What we need is someone to be an advocate for these children," she said. "I have taught children like this before and had no idea how to help them. We need teachers to be more aware, to get some training in dealing with language disorder."

Claire sat bolt upright in her chair. I had got to know her over the year and I knew her to be a person of action. When she makes up her mind to do something, it gets done. Her determination had passed itself on to Joshy and he had shown the same kind of strength. The day he said "myself" to me, and decided to say complete sentences on his own, without help, was the day I knew him to be his mother's son. And it was clear now that Claire had 'An Idea'.

"Before I had kids I was a lawyer," she said. "If anyone can do advocacy, it's me!"

And so the Language Project started. Claire and I agreed to meet once a week, and to collect any information on S.L.I. available online or in libraries. She would then start a campaign with posters and talks to schools. I could do teacher training sessions, and she could talk from her personal experience as Joshy's mum.

Our main message would be: This boy is not stupid, he is not lazy, he is not naughty. He has specific language impairment.

Claire

I had been feeling restless for months. I had always been sure I would go back to work as soon as Joshy started nursery, but with all his difficulties and those dreadful sleepless months I kept putting it off. But now that he was going to be in school all day I needed to do something with my time. So Nan's idea about advocacy was just perfect. As soon as she said it I felt that it was just made for me. I am known (ask Dave!) to be an articulate person, and to be confident speaking in public. Which was one of the things which made it even sadder for me to think about Joshy, so competent in so many ways, but whose one area of weakness was in talking.

But what could be better than for me to use my gift to support him, and kids like him?

I got home from that school meeting on a high. I started thinking: we would need business cards, letterheads, and a logo. I started a file to collect newspaper cuttings about special education, so that I would have names of people already writing on this topic. I put together a list of local schools, and of people running voluntary organisations providing learning support in schools. I had long ago started another file for all the information I had read on the internet about S.L.I., and now I went through it again and tried to summarise the main points so that I would be able to explain it to people.

Dave was keen to be involved and helped me to clear a corner of the study so there would be a dedicated space for the new project. And I explained to Jenna and Joshy, hopefully in a way he could understand, that I would be coming to the school sometimes to talk to the teachers and to talk to other mummies and daddies whose children needed speech therapy. Joshy seemed indifferent and I don't know if he understood, but I thought it only fair to tell him. Jenna was initially embarrassed that I might come and talk in her class and I am sorry to say that I got rather pious and self-righteous and told her to think of other people sometimes, not just of herself, and how would she like it if she had a language disorder and couldn't talk?

Of course afterwards I felt guilty at having lost my temper and not having handled Jenna's feelings well.

I know how it feels to be embarrassed by your parents; I had often been embarrassed by mine. I was simply upset because Jenna was throwing cold water on my idea and ruining my excitement. But actually, dealing with her comment was a good trial run. I knew I would have to learn to deal with questions, with people being irritated by me, with a widespread lack of understanding of S.L.I.

If advocacy was easy, more people would be doing it.

I looked it up on the internet: 'Advocacy: The act of pleading or arguing in favour of something, such as a cause, idea, or policy; active support.' I also found, in the thesaurus, lots of equivalent words: support, championing, backing, promoting, campaigning for, becoming a spokesman for.

I found that in the U.K. there are organisations which actually print leaflets explaining to parents how to become advocates for their child with language disorder.

There were a few courses available to train people in advocacy here in South Africa, but these dealt with much weightier, life-and-death issues: AIDS awareness, the right to running water and electricity, women's rights. All of which were such pressing issues that I had a moment when I wondered if I was making a fuss about nothing. Our own lives were so privileged, compared to the lives of people who still lived in appalling conditions in the townships.

But I got over that thought quite quickly. My child's right to language was one of the most important things for Joshy himself and for our family. Joshy, and kids like him, have at the very least a right to be heard. Making a bit of a fuss so that teachers would get additional training could only be a good thing. And becoming an example to my own children of how to stand up for personal rights was something I felt very strongly about. There would be no shrinking violets in this family.

So I would make up my own advocacy training course. I had had enough practice over the past four years, just going through all those doctors' appointments and the occupational therapy and the swimming lessons, and helping Joshy through his first years at school and his first year of speech therapy.

Joshy

I got a new teacher, no more Nan, my new teacher name is Yasmine. No more nursery school. I now in 'ception and Yasmine is teacher in 'ception.

I got new books, new pencil, new pencil case, new school cap.

Mummy says I going to learn to read. I want to read, Jenna can read and she gets homework and I want homework. I want to take books home and read books. I want to write words like Jenna.

Today we did letters.

aaa eee mmmm ssss

Yasmine tells us stand up and say your name, how old are you, where do you live.

I know my name, Joshy. I know how old, 5. I can't remember where I live. Maybe number 62, maybe number 26. The children laugh. Yasmine say sit down Joshy.

I wish it was Nan my teacher.

CHAPTER 20

Nili

After a day or two, Joshy was able to find his way to his new class with confidence. It was still summer and the classrooms were quite hot, and I thought that being cooped up all day in a hot room, with an unfamiliar teacher who was teaching these five-year-olds in a rather more formal manner than when they were at nursery, would be quite difficult for Joshy, but he seemed calm and relaxed when I went to his classroom to fetch him for his speech therapy sessions.

Now that Joshy's teacher was starting to teach the children to read and write, I needed to start work on a new area: phonological awareness. This was something I would ideally like to have started earlier, but there was so much work to be done on his listening and understanding and talking, that this had had to wait.

What phonological awareness means is knowing how to listen to, to notice and to isolate the sounds in words. Even if the child does not yet know which letters represent which sounds, he should be able to hear that in a word like 'dog' there are three different sounds, which can be said separately: d, o, g. If I broke the word into its sounds and said the three sounds (not their letter names, just the sounds) separately, a child should, around the age of four, be able to tell me what my word is.

Phonological awareness also involves things like being able to break longer words into their syllables or beats (e-le-phant is three beats, Jo-shy is two, dog is one). It also refers to the ability to hear which words rhyme with each other. No matter how a word is spelled, a child with good phonological awareness will know that 'bite' and 'right' (in the song about 'which finger did he bite') both sound the same at the end of the word. Children with good phonological awareness know that book and bat both start with the same sound, even if they don't yet know that the letter 'b' is the way to write down that sound.

These are the kinds of things which children with normal language development pick up very early, through listening to nursery rhymes, and through talking and understanding. What makes phonological awareness a complicated idea is that this kind of understanding or awareness has nothing to do with writing or reading – it is about the careful listening to, noticing and remembering of sounds. But without this awareness, writing and reading become a dauntingly difficult task.

And children with language impairment usually find this a huge mountain to climb. Hearing and remembering the differences between sounds, remembering in which order sounds appear in a word, remembering two different sounds and comparing them to each other, are often precisely the things which a child with S.L.I. cannot do.

I needed urgently to start this kind of work with Joshy to prepare him for reading. My real worry was that having come such a long way with his confidence and his understanding and talking, he would now start to find the challenge of learning to read and spell too difficult, and would lose his hard-won self-assurance.

The worst outcome would not be that he struggled to read, but that he would become again that silent worried Joshy whom I had met seven months earlier.

* * *

I didn't want to launch straight in to something new and difficult so we did some storytelling first. Then I took out a box with some pictures which I had prepared. I had two groups of pictures: words which started with M (moon, man, mouse, money) and words which started with S (sea, seal, soap, sun, sky). I chose those two sounds because they are very different from each other in terms of what the mouth has to do to produce them, and also because they are very visible if a listener is looking at a speaker saying those words. These two sounds also happened to be two of the first letters Joshy's teacher Yasmine was going to be teaching in class.

"We are going to listen to a sound. The sound is M. Mmmmmmmm. Can you say it?"

"Mmmmm", said Joshy, "easy peasy!"

I took out the small mirror, and showed him what we do with our mouth to say mmm.

"Here is a word," I said, showing him the picture of the moon. "Mmmoon! Can you hear it? It starts with mmmm. Moon. Mmmmoon. Mmmoon."

I took out our posting box, an empty tissue box, covered on all sides in lovely red paper with the slot for the tissues cut out, so that Joshy could post the pictures through it into the letterbox.

"Here's a game. If you hear a word with mmm, you can post it in the box."

I picked up the picture of the man. "Mmmmman," I said, exaggerating the M to make it clear to Joshy that he must listen to the first sound of the word. "Mmman. Has it got mmm?"

"Yes," said Joshy, and took the picture and posted it in the letterbox. I did the same with 'mouse.' Then I picked up the picture of the seal. "Sssseal," I said. "Does it start with mmm?"

He took the picture and put it in the letterbox. We clearly had a long way to go.

Claire

I asked my niece, who is a graphic designer, to help me develop a logo and think of a catchy name for the S.L.I. advocacy project. We tried lots of names: Help2Talk, Learn to Talk, Talk To Me, but decided they were all too one-sided. We wanted something which would represent not just the talking, but also how people listen to each other. We threw ideas back and forth and came up with 'P.A.L.S.': an acronym for Promoting Awareness of Language delay in Schools. I can't remember whose idea it actually was, it was one of those things which just happen when two people are thinking together.

We had toyed with Awareness of Language Delay. But the acronym would then have been A.L.D., too clumsy to say, and too similar to A.S.D. (autistic spectrum disorder) or to A.D.H.D. (attention deficit and hyperactivity disorder).

Children with either of these conditions might also have language delay, as I well knew from all my internet searches, and we wanted to be specific about our project, and not include all the many other causes of language delay. Though we worried about that for a while too. How could we exclude those kids, when so many of the ideas which speech therapists use must be useful for them too?

But when we asked around and did some internet searching and found out how much awareness and support there already was for kids with A.S.D. and A.D.H.D., we decided to stick with P.A.L.S. and to support kids like Joshy, with S.L.I.

We got to like the name P.A.L.S. It seemed to make sense. If you have language, you can have pals, and you can talk to your friends. So after that it was quite easy to come up with a logo which showed some children talking to each other, being pals.

We put together a letterhead with the logo and my email address on it. Now I was ready. All I had to do now (all? This was going to be the hardest part!) was to get out there: to talk to people, to raise awareness, to get the support of parents and schools and teachers, and of the Education Department, and to get speech therapists on board to help out in giving talks, writing articles, preparing posters.

I was starting to realise the size of the project I had taken on.

Joshy's head teacher was wonderful. Not only did she immediately start planning some teacher training sessions at her school, but she also wrote a letter explaining what we were doing and sent it to the Head Teachers' Newsletter, which is circulated to all schools in the Cape Province.

Nili and I wrote a leaflet, explaining, on one side of the leaflet, what S.L.I is, and on the other side introducing P.A.L.S. and offering to come and talk to teachers. We made fifty copies and we sent a leaflet to all the schools in Cape Town.

I gathered up all my courage and phoned the local newspaper and asked them to put me through to the reporter who dealt with family affairs and education. It was surprisingly easy to get through to her on the phone and to arrange a meeting. I rushed through printing the business cards and letterheads, and I put together a presentation with some of the most clearly written and concise information I had collected, so that by the time

I met the reporter I had something solid to give her and to tell her. She suggested that I contact the local talk radio as well.

At the end of the week I was on a high. I felt full of energy, really quite powerful, and Dave was as excited as I was. We felt that this was education by example. I was showing Joshy and Jenna that when you have a problem you don't sit down and wait for it to go away, you get up and do something about it.

* * *

But picking up Joshy from school on Friday, after his first week in Reception Class, quickly brought me down to earth. I asked Yasmine how he was doing. She showed me his writing book.

I don't know how to describe it. He had written pages and pages of letters but they didn't stay on the line, they were not the same size, and they became increasingly illegible. By the second page there was print all over the page but nothing made any sense and everything sloped downwards, as if he had turned his book sideways to write.

His maths book was no better – Yasmine explained that she had focused on getting him to distinguish 5 from 2, and then 6 from 9. He was reversing all the letters and numbers that resembled each other, something I knew he had difficulty with. The page was filled with scrawled shapes of different sizes, some of which looked like nothing recognisable at all. And when I asked her if Nan had explained Joshy's language delay to her, she said, "Oh yes, I know about it, I have taught children with language problems before, but that is nothing to do with his writing, surely?"

I was stumped. I didn't know the answer, and, with a sinking heart, started to think that maybe he had other problems as well, which we hadn't realised until now. I didn't know what to say to her and anyway there were other parents about, and they all wanted some time with Yasmine, so I took Joshy home.

Joshy

Yasmine give us a book for writing. I like writing, I got homework like Jenna. I can write what I see on the board.

I write all down the whole page and I write all down the next page. I write lots. Yasmine give us a book for maths. I don't know five and two, I did it wrong, Yasmine say it not right.

This is my writing.

llllllllllllllllllllllllllllll

iiiiiiiiiiiiiiiiiiiiiiiiiiiiiiiiiii

oooooooooooooooooooooooooo

My story.

A dinosaur drive in a new car. He got new car, got new fire engine.

He go driving long way, far away from Cape Town, over the sea. He go driving up Table Mountain, go driving to Boulders Beach, have a picnic in the car.

Then he go home. Then he go to the shop. He buy new book, new pencil, new pencil case. All them new things, he got them.

He go to sleep in the night. He a happy dinosaur, smiling.

CHAPTER 21

Nili

We continued to work on learning to notice and isolate the first sound of a word, the sound a word starts with. I asked Joshy just to listen, and gave him the pictures of words which start with M. We put them all in a little box and I wrote 'M' on the lid. Then I took the words starting with S and said them aloud to him, exaggerating the S. I handed him the pictures and a box and he put the S words in the box. I wrote 'S' on the lid.

Then I took them all out, put them in a heap on the table, and said, "Let's make a milkshake! Mix mix mix!" And we mixed up all the pictures. "Now let's put them back, M in this box, S in this box. Help me Joshy, they're all mixed up."

I picked up one picture at a time, at random, and exaggerated the first sound, and asked him to copy my word, to say it in the way I was saying it, and to put it in the correct box. It took a lot of help for him to sort the pictures into their two boxes.

This was painstakingly slow work. Initially Joshy didn't understand 'first' as in 'the first sound'. He knew the word 'first' to mean the person who wins a race. So I drew a train with a steam engine and two coaches and showed him that the engine is first. I had to show Joshy that the first one is the one on the left, as we read from left to right in English. He did not know left or right, so that took a bit of time.

The next coach was in the middle, and the last coach was at the end of the train. I had to show him that *first*, and *at the beginning*, and *starts with*, all mean the same thing when you are talking about the sounds in a word; he knew that *last* and *at the end* mean the same thing but I had to explain to him that a sound can be last without being the loser of a race.

Learning language is difficult.

When I thought about the size of the task ahead of us I have to admit I was feeling a bit discouraged. We would have to do this with every sound in the alphabet. And even once Josh had learned to recognise the letters S, H, and C, and say their sounds, he would have to relearn them all over again for SH and CH, which in spite of being made up of familiar written letters, suddenly had completely different spoken sounds when they were joined together.

And I could already see how difficult it was for him to remember which letters represented which sounds. Even after I had let him write M's all over a page, and we had said the sound over and over, and closed our eyes and listened to the sound, and looked at and said the name of the pictures of the words starting with the sound, as soon as I added words with S and then went back to M, Joshy got confused.

Reading difficulties are known to be an aspect of S.L.I. for many children, and I had always suspected that Joshy would need much more coaching and repetition than the other children in the class if he was ever to learn which letters corresponded to which sounds. I made a mental note to tell Claire to include reading difficulties in the information she was collecting about S.L.I.

* * *

The sad thing was that Joshy was starting to realise that he was not learning in the way the other children in his class were learning. Yasmine told me that he did not put his hand up when she asked a question, and that no matter how many times the teaching assistant went over the letters and sounds with him, he seemed to know them one day and forget them the next.

I was determined to continue our work on language, and not only on phonological awareness, even though this was his most pressing need in class. So we did some work on vocabulary. We played a game called 'What does not belong' in which three pictures of objects from one category (for example animals) are placed together with one picture from a different category (for example buildings). Joshy had to tell me which picture did not belong in the group, and why it did not belong. This meant he had not only to know that a house is different from lions and elephants (which of course he knew) but had to be able to tell me that lion, elephant and giraffe go together because they are all *animals*, but house does not belong because it is a kind of *building*. We had played this game many times before and Joshy enjoyed it as it stretched him just enough to help him learn new words, but did not make him feel a failure. We moved on to more complex ideas.

I gave him the task of adding to the game by choosing new pictures to cut out of magazines, so that we would not be working with the same categories over and over. This was a lot harder as Joshy had to think up a category and find three examples, and then think of a different category and choose one example. We used catalogues from department stores and supermarkets, and found a stationery page (stapler, ruler, banana, hole punch: which one does not belong?) and that was fun because Joshy enjoyed learning the words for stapler and hole punch.

We found a fruit and vegetable page and that was a challenge for me because I had to try to work out whether a tomato is a fruit or a vegetable, and explain to Joshy the difference between a vegetable and a fruit. I realised that I actually had no idea. Do vegetables only grow in the ground? Are fruits things that grow on trees and have seeds? So is tomato then a fruit or a vegetable? And what about gooseberries, which grow on a bush, not too different from tomato bushes?

Joshy was giggling. He enjoyed seeing me struggle, and I exaggerated my confusion a bit so that he could get the full benefit of seeing that adults sometimes struggle to explain things too. And I loved the way he relaxed and lost his frown lines. But they soon returned when he tried to say 'vegetable' and could only manage 'veggible'. I broke the word into its syllables and simplified it from ve-ge-ta-ble (four syllables) to veg-ta-ble (three) but he still struggled: Vettible. Veggible. Vegital. Fenchible. And then he put his head down on the desk and just gave in to his sadness.

Claire

Joshy had been showing more and more interest in watching birds since Nili had lent him a book about local bird life. He thought it was hilarious that the book tried to describe, in writing, what the bird calls sound like. "Read to me, what it say for robin?" I would read the strange syllables which the book's author thought he heard in each bird's call: "Tu tu tu tweeee." "Sirrup, sirrup, sirrup." Joshy would laugh uproariously. "That bird not say sirrup! Nobody say sirrup, only in the kitchen you say sirrup for pancake!" Nili suggested a family game, which might encourage Joshy to listen to sounds and to identify letters: we would each choose a bird's call and try to imitate it, and then we would help him to look it up in the book and see what it said.

It was a perfect way for Joshy to practice his reading, as the bird calls were always written in short syllables, sounding out exactly, phonetically, what the written letters said, with none of the bizarre vowel or consonant combinations that written English uses.

Nili had told me what she called a speech therapy joke: the way to spell 'fish' is 'ghoti': 'gh' is read as 'f' in a word like 'rough'; 'o' is read as 'i' in a word like 'women'; and 'ti' is read as 'sh' in a word like 'emotion.' She was trying to show me that in reading English there seem to be more exceptions than rules.

I didn't think it was funny.

At Joshy's request we started having family picnics in Kirstenbosch, the huge botanical garden near our house. His favourite birds were guinea fowls (he could now say the word, with a more-or-less acceptable G) and hadedas, a kind of ibis, who, with their tiny heads, over-sized beaks and massive wingspan looked more like prehistoric monsters than birds, and who produced loud, manic cries when they flew. And even though Dave's and my personal preferences were for something a bit more energetic, like cycling and swimming, we learned to sit still, to watch and to listen, like Joshy.

Perhaps I was reading too much into it, but I wondered if his love of these loud birds came from his own difficulties in saying what he was thinking, in speaking up and making his presence felt? Certainly these birds, with no words or sentences, used their voices loud and clear to tell everyone who they were.

I knew that in some ways, Joshy was possibly going to miss out on things which I have always taken for granted: reading good fiction (I love detective novels), the quick, witty, sarcastic banter, the subtle wordplays which Dave and I enjoy, and which Jenna was starting to pick up on. But I was determined that in spite of this, Joshy would have a life of excitement and variety and interest.

I wanted him to develop interests of his own, to develop expertise in any field or activity he chose, and that included his love of surfing, as well as his fascination with all the creepy crawlies who live at the seashore, and his new interest in birds.

We spent hours after school and on weekends at the beach. When he was not surfing, or if it was too cold to go in the water, he would sit on the beach at the water's edge digging for clams and whelks, and later, at home, he would frantically look for their pictures in the sea life books he had chosen at the library, so that he could see illustrations of the things he had found, and study them in detail. I sometimes found it hard to reconcile the screaming, nervous baby, and the exhaustion of my first months with him, with this curious, fascinated and fascinating person who was Joshy.

* * *

And yet when I read the stories in his exercise book, I was struck by a new sadness in his stories, a new sense of hopelessness, which seemed to be emerging. I felt so sorry for the snake who was little and begging for attention, and for the butterfly who worked so hard to fly and in the end died anyway. I wondered if Joshy felt that his life at school was all just too much effort. Did he wonder why we were making him work so hard?

When I talked to Dave about it he said he had also thought of that but didn't want to upset me; and anyway, he said, I suppose Joshy's stories show that he is a bit of a philosopher, because yes, life can be lots of effort, and bad things sometimes happen, but aren't there some lovely bits in life too? So we decided to just enjoy Joshy's interests and his excitement in whatever he was learning, whether at school or out of school.

And after those initial difficult first weeks in class he was now starting to copy letters more accurately, and even though he did not know what they stood for I could see he was enjoying a feeling of mastery simply by being able to write them neatly, accurately, over and over and over.

Joshy

Nili got animals in her bag. Big snake and little snake. I got a story. One snake is big and one snake small.

Little snake say to big snake, can I sit on your tail?

No!! you not sit on my tail.

Little snake say, can I sit on your head?

No! Get away! Shoo!

Can I sit on your back?"

No! Go away, you can't do nothing!"

Little snake say where can I go?

Big snake say, "Go back in box".

***

Butterfly coming.

He singing. I can fly! I can fly!

I flying little bit high. I fly more high.

I flying higher and higher and higher.

And tumble down, and he not fly.

Then he dead.

***

The dinosaur want to grab the house, grab the car.

He kick it, he go out.

Then he go up up up. Then he gone.

CHAPTER 22

Nili

In the weeks that followed I saw a Joshy who was becoming increasingly despondent. The frown lines between his eyes were back, and watching him in the classroom it became clear that he was becoming more silent, and was keeping his head down in that old posture I remembered from his first year. Yasmine was doing her best to adapt the work for him so that he could cope, but we both knew he was falling way behind. On one hand, Claire was telling me how much Joshy was learning at home, how he was developing his knowledge and passion for wildlife and birds, and on the other hand here was a Joshy who seemed to be getting quieter and sadder with each passing week at school.

Sometimes he would come to a speech therapy session and just sit there, not speaking. I tried to imagine how he must be feeling, but really I could only guess.

The teachers were planning a one-day strike in the coming week. Teachers were increasingly struggling to pay their bills with the fast-rising cost of living, and their salaries had not changed in four years. Joshy knew that "Next week Tuesday no school" but had not understood what a strike meant. So I explained it in simple words: Teachers need some more money. The people who give them money said no. So the teachers are a bit upset and they will not come to work on Tuesday. Maybe the people who pay them money will be sad and ask them to come back to school and will give them money.

"That is a new word, a strike. A strike is like what you feel when your words don't come to your mouth; your words sometimes go on strike and the words don't work."

He sat up and looked straight at me, for the first time in the session. I went on: "Joshy, sometimes your words will go on strike, and it's alright, I don't mind. If your words are on strike, if your words don't want to talk, we can still play lots of games here, we can play games with no words. Would you like that?"

The smoothing out of his frown lines gave me my answer. I never thought I would find a teachers' strike so helpful.

I spoke to Claire about reducing our two sessions a week and going back to one, so that Joshy could have one session with the school's specialist reading teacher and one with me. Claire and I decided to go together to the head teacher to talk about this, and also to fill her in on the way the Language Project was developing, and to finalise the dates for my teacher training sessions with all the teachers in the Early Years department.

* * *

When I took Joshy for his second session that week, I went back to some of the listening activities we had done last term, which were now 'easy peasy' for him. I wanted to remind him of his confident self and to see a smile instead of his frown lines. And he did relax for a while. But when I said, "Let's do some letters," he just collapsed. It was as if a balloon had been deflated.

He put his head down on the table and would not say a word. I spoke to him about how he was good at surfing, and that most of the children in his class didn't know how to surf. I talked to him about how he knew the names of lots of birds and even what sound they made, and that most of the children in his class didn't know anything about birds.

I tried to tell him, it's not your fault. Some people are good at some things, like surfing and birds, but they are not so good at reading. And some people think reading is 'easy peasy,' but they can't surf. I am here to help you with talking, and your new reading teacher will help you with reading, and you can be good at those things too, but we have to wait a while. We have to be patient. I told him I knew it was hard, but we would help him.

I wondered again whether Joshy should have a break from speech therapy for a term or so, and concentrate solely on his reading. My worst fears were being realised, and over the last two months he had started to lose all his hard-won confidence. His bouncy, confident walk, and the smiley face, which I had become accustomed to seeing when he came into my room, were somehow diminished, and his face was now solemn, his frown lines appearing frequently, his head down. It felt as if he had, by the end of the previous school year, briefly found that the world of school was a lovely place to be, and now he was seeing that actually it was not that lovely. I decided to wait a few weeks before making any drastic decisions about having a break from speech therapy.

* * *

I thought a lot about Joshy's silence. When we first started to work together I felt, as did Nan and Claire at the time, that his silence was like an imprisonment, that he was desperate to break out of it, to talk and play with other children, and that learning to talk would set him free. And indeed, towards the end of that first period of our work together, he increasingly became one of the class, playing and talking with groups of children in the playground.

But this new silence was different – it was a silence of sadness. He was now old enough to realise that what others did with ease, he could not do. I felt he was on the verge of giving up on himself.

This was something which was not mentioned in the beautiful book about silence, by Sara Maitland, which I was reading at the time. The author was an accomplished, assertive, articulate writer who had decided to choose silence as a way of living, in order to lead a more contemplative life. She wanted to spend time thinking, praying, and observing life around her, rather than speaking. Joshy did not have this choice. Both his silences, the terrified one and the despondent one, were something imposed upon him by his language disorder.

If I think about myself, on balance I do usually prefer silence to talk. My choice of how to spend my spare time is to be in places where there is mostly silence – in the garden, or out watching birds, or just sitting in the sun drinking tea and not talking. Away from traffic, away from large groups of people, avoiding dinner parties if possible, never going to the beach in the holidays when it is crowded.

Years ago, after a particularly difficult period at work, I decided to go on a weekend silent retreat. But when I saw how expensive it was I decided to do the retreat at home. I explained to Vito, and he was not thrilled at the prospect of spending a weekend with me when I didn't talk to him, but he understood the idea behind it and even helped by offering to be silent too. We did quite well on Saturday, but on Sunday morning Vito was making toasted sandwiches and I tried to explain that I wanted the tomatoes sliced very thin, and one slice of onion, and brown bread not white, and no pepper, and he just could not understand my gestures. And anyway the point of silent retreats is not to use gesture or sign language but to be silent. So it became silly and pointless and we laughed and we ended the silent retreat then and there. But it did give me a taste of what Joshy and others like him with S.L.I. might feel, the frustration, the feeling of just wanting to give up and turn away.

I had the choice. For Joshy, the silence was not a choice.

When I was a teenager I used to worry about my preference for silence, in fact I was a bit embarrassed by it, and thought I should work on being more outgoing, more of an extrovert. But mercifully, as I got older I started to accept that that's how I am, and in fact I like being this way. But what I wanted for Joshy was that he would be able to make that choice too, and decide how much of his day he preferred to spend alone with his hobbies and thoughts, perhaps just surfing, which is essentially a solo activity, and how much he wanted to be with friends and family, talking and communicating.

Joshy

I drawed a picture. I drawed a alien. He got spiky hair and three eyes. He got big big feet, he got long shoes.

He got eleven arms and antennas on his head on his back on his shoulders. He got buttons on his shirt on his arms on his legs. Also- spiky fingers.

A scary alien. He say, I want to eat some people. Who can I eat? Boy says, you can't eat me, go away alien! Then monkey says, you can't eat me, go away!

So alien went out of the house. Goodbye alien.

Nili said, do you want to tell me a story. No. Got no more story.

CHAPTER 23

Nili

Now that phonological awareness and letters were being worked on by the specialist reading teacher, Anne, I could stop working on those areas and focus again on language work. I wanted to revise Joshy's use of personal pronouns: he and she, his and hers, to him and to her. He still got these wrong, sometimes saying he instead of she, and saying things like 'I give it to she' instead of 'I give it to her', or 'it is he book' instead of 'it is his book'.

We worked with male and female puppets; we told stories about them (*he* likes playing football, *she* likes surfing) we gave them birthday presents (he is giving a surfboard *to her*; she is giving a chocolate *to him*) and we described their clothes (*his* hat is green, *her* shoes are pink). Sometimes Joshy got it right and sometimes he made mistakes. We did this for three weeks, until he suddenly gathered up all the puppets, put them in the box and closed the box firmly.

"*It doesn't matter!*" he said. "Why it matter? You *know* I mean him, you *know* I mean this one (pointing to the girl puppet), it doesn't matter what I call it. I look at this one, I mean this one! I look at that one, I mean that one! You *know* what I mean!"

Joshy was impressive when he got cross, and logically his argument made sense. How much did it really matter if his personal pronouns were mixed up? I usually did know what he meant when he told me about things that happened at home, about himself or his sister. And if I didn't know who he was referring to, I could ask.

I tried to explain to him why it mattered, and told him a story about when I had wanted to buy a present for my daughter, and if I had told the shop assistant 'he likes sport' the shop assistant would have wanted to sell me a football. So my lovely clever Joshy said, "Whatsa difference, girls play football, boys play football, it's the same!"

But clever as his argument was, I kept thinking about something I had read in one of Adam Phillips' books: that for a child to talk about what he really wants and needs and believes, he needs to risk being humiliated, to risk exposing himself. And for someone like Joshy, who had only recently found his voice, I thought how hard it must be to risk using that new and fragile instrument to stand up for what he believed, with adults who would always be more powerful, who would be better at using language and who could always argue more strongly.

So just the fact that he was arguing with me about language was, for Joshy, a wonderful step forward. And even though I could see how upset he was, I was at the same time secretly really pleased, because this was the Joshy I loved to see, the tough boy who could stand up for himself. So I said to him, "O.K., maybe you are right, let me think about it for a while. Let's do something else today."

Clearly I had some work to do if I was going to be able to convince him that personal pronouns were worth spending our precious therapy time on, when we could be doing storytelling and making longer and longer sentences – something he was always willing to work on. He was now able to join sentences with 'and', with 'because', with 'so that.' He insisted that I count the words in his sentences and write down how many words he had used in each sentence, and we celebrated his long sentences with high-fives.

He was still enjoying seeing that his ideas and stories were important enough for me to write them down in his book, and he knew from this activity that print is not just something which you struggle to learn in class, but something which lets you keep your stories safe, so that you, and other people too, can read them later.

* * *

Now that he had been in therapy for eight months I decided it was time to try out some formal assessments, which I had not been able to use when he was so fearful of talking last year. The assessments were needed so that he could continue to get speech therapy at the school, as only those children with demonstrated language delay were eligible for therapy. The alternative was for Claire to take Joshy to therapy after school, in the afternoons, and we were really reluctant to add to his busy day, or to have him miss out on some of his outings and play dates.

I met with Claire and Dave to give them feedback about the assessments. It was a very difficult meeting, because on one hand there had been such wonderful changes in his language as well as his behaviour and his social skills, and on the other hand he was having such a hard time at school. I was optimistic about his work with the reading teacher but I had to write down, in black and white, on the speech and language therapy report, his actual language levels for understanding and talking, and he was still scoring very low on all the tests.

"So what is the future for him?" asked Dave quietly. "Will he always be behind the rest of the class? Will he learn to read and write? Will he even finish school?" It was a sober moment.

S.L.I. does not just go away. But these children do make wonderful progress with the right kind of teaching, with specialist reading teachers, and speech therapy, and they continue to make progress right through their school careers. The main thing was to keep going, to take the long view, and to make sure that Joshy grew up to be a person who was confident in his ability to think, to plan, to express his wishes, and to reach his potential. That meant encouraging his strengths. His swimming, his surfing, his growing love of bird watching and of wildlife. There is more to life than school, was what I wanted to say to this family.

And even though all through my long career in speech therapy, and in my spare time too, I have been involved with and fascinated by language and communication, I do know, and truly believe, that some things matter more.

The meeting ended with Claire crying, and then apologising for crying, and Dave trying to explain that he really did appreciate all we were doing for Joshy, but we all left the meeting with a heavy heart.

Claire

I was feeling optimistic after having met the specialist reading teacher, Anne, who was warm and gentle and who I was sure Joshy would feel comfortable with. She was going to give him the one lesson a week to which the head teacher had agreed, but she also very generously offered, in her own time, to come in twice a week for half an hour in the morning before school started, so that Joshy wouldn't miss too much of his classroom time.

He took to her immediately, and became determined to read. I know that look and the way he sets his chin, and unlike any child I have ever met, he started to come home from school and go straight into his reading homework, actually refusing to go outside until he had done it.

***

Joshy's language had come on in leaps and bounds, but when Dave and I came to the meeting with Nili to hear the results of the language assessment, we walked in with dread in our hearts. I was already on the verge of tears before we arrived, so it didn't take much for me to actually start to cry when Nili showed us that although Joshy had made wonderful progress, he was still far from being at the level expected for children his age. His understanding was still very delayed, and his spoken grammar and vocabulary were still at least a year behind the level of most children of his age.

Nili pointed out a few times (she could see how upset I was) that these average measures thrown up by formal tests do not show how much progress he had made, nor did they show that his storytelling was really very good, even though his grammar was not yet that good. He was now able to tell a story, using past tense, and introducing characters and events; he was able to ask questions, to refuse to do things, to explain what he meant, express his ideas and feelings about things. All of this is what language is for, she explained, and he can do this.

But Dave and I could see that there was no quick fix, and not even a slow fix. Almost a whole year of therapy and Joshy still had problems.

Joshy

My long sentence. I got lot of words:

The boy like to surf so then he going surfing with he sister she also like to surf and she got a pink shoes because she a girl. She like pink and it was she birthday so she got a present it is pink shoes and a pink surfboard and a pink bicycle.

I got all them words. I got 28 words and I got 25 words!

* * *

This is story about a alien.

"I want to eat some people!! Who can I eat!"

I say to him, "You not eat me! Go away alien! Pow!! I punching you aliens! No eat me, cause I stronger. Go away!"

The alien went out of my house. Goodbye! No come back!"

CHAPTER 24

Nili

After more than a month of intensive work, three times a week, Anne, the specialist reading teacher, started to see real progress in Joshy's reading. He started to take home little reading books and proudly telling people about the books that he could read.

Because Joshy loved these little story books, and still loved our sessions in the drama tent when he made up stories and I wrote them down for him, I decided to continue using stories as a basis for our language work. We also started to work on scripts, which Claire had been using at home to talk about their outings, and I chose activities which we could do and complete in a single session, at school.

So our first script was about making fruit salad. I brought some fruit, two knives, a chopping board, and a big salad bowl, and we washed the fruit, cut it up, and made a delicious salad. I took photos of each step in the process, and after we had eaten our fruit salad I took Joshy with me to the school secretary's office and asked for a special favour: to print out the pictures from my phone.

We had twelve pictures, and we stuck them on a big page, in their correct order. Joshy numbered each picture and then told the story. "This is how to make fruit salad. Number one, first you wash the fruit. Picture number two, then you cut it in pieces..."

Over the next few weeks we made a model airplane, a kite, furniture from matchboxes, and a monster made of tin foil baking dishes cut into rectangles, with eyes made of sewing machine bobbins and hands made of string with plumbing washers. Joshy loved this kind of work, learned new words, talked and talked and talked, and didn't go on strike once. It was a really good period for us.

But in class Yasmine was finding it really difficult to teach him. She had adapted some of the work he did, so that he could learn at his own pace, but this meant that he worked with the teaching assistant for many hours, in one corner of the classroom, and was becoming increasingly separated from his classmates.

His maths was coming on but he needed everything to be made really concrete, with counters and bottle tops and an abacus, while the other children were more and more able to understand ideas about maths which used language, and did not need props or objects.

This is so often a problem for children with S.L.I. Even with lots of teaching and therapy they continue to struggle to understand abstract language. And as he was already getting extra help with reading, and with me, how much more extra help could the school provide?

And surely taking him out of the class for extra lessons would make him feel more isolated rather than less? It was impossible to answer these questions. Every option seemed to have its good points and its bad points.

This was a dilemma most teachers have to deal with – a child who can't cope with the work, but who would become socially excluded if provided with a special teacher and an adapted curriculum. It was hard to know how to arrange things in a way which would be most fair to Joshy, and still not affect the other children in the class. In the end Yasmine asked Claire and Dave to decide how much time, and in which subjects, they would prefer him to be working on an adapted curriculum with the teaching assistant, and Yasmine said she would make sure that he would rejoin the class for sport, gym, singing and science.

Claire

Joshy started to read. We were thrilled for him, especially since we all knew how hard he had worked at it and how he had not given up, even though it must have been one of the most difficult things he had ever done. But there was also something else I felt – something which I can only call triumph. At last people were starting to believe in Joshy, to give him his chance to shine.

And even though I had not forgotten his early months and years, those times of exhaustion, dread, worry, and a whole lot of other awful things, once he started sleeping and eating normally I just knew that this boy would one day be able to do anything he set his mind to, and that all the negative responses he was getting from my family and friends and from teachers at school were wrong: that they would one day see what this boy could do. And now, between his class teachers and his reading teacher and Nili and our family, he had reached this point.

He had been bringing home little reading books and insisted on reading to us, as well as to my mum on the phone. He would read the same book, over and over and over.

In spite of our very real happiness at his starting to read, I also felt a bit guilty as I grew increasingly bored with the little books in which not much happened. Why was Joshy not bored? Did he actually understand what he was reading?

I decided to try to find out. I took a piece of cardboard and cut a horizontal slot, which was approximately the size of the words he was reading. I covered up the whole page and let one word at a time peep out through the slot. Now that the whole sentence was covered up, Joshy had to really know how to read each word on its own. He managed to read 'dog' and 'a', but could not read most of the other words: he, the, once, tail.

This was in spite of the fact that he could go through these books in a flash, reading every sentence perfectly.

So I suddenly realised that he was simply memorising the sentences and using the lovely pictures on each page to help himself to 'read', but that actually in each book he could only read perhaps two or three words. And even though Nili had told me (several times) that children at this age should not really have to learn to read, it's a bit young, he could have waited until he was six, I knew what the other kids in his class were doing because I had made it my business to go and have a look.

I panicked and phoned Anne, the reading teacher. She was lovely; so understanding, so patient. She knew that he was memorising some sentences but she showed me that that is a part of normal reading and she showed me how much progress he had made. I asked her to give me ideas how to help Joshy at home, so we photocopied the little books he had been reading and enlarged the print. We cut out the words and stuck them on cards and put them in a box, which I covered with beautiful paper. She showed me how to use them as flashcards: I could ask Joshy to read a word on a card and then to find that word in his reading book, or to read a sentence in his reading book and then look for the words on the cards and make the same sentence on the table, using the cards.

She also explained to me that there are some 'high frequency words' which can't be decoded even if you do know your letters and sounds perfectly (which Joshy didn't). Words like 'the' and 'friend' are not pronounced anything like the way they are written; you can't sound them out and work out what the word is, so you just have to remember it, and that is the problem with English. Some languages, she told me, like Italian, are much easier to learn to read, because most words are written just as they are spoken – much like the bird sounds in our bird books. "English is one of the hardest languages to learn to read if you have language delay," she told me. Huh. Great. We should have moved from the U.K. to Italy, not to South Africa.

Joshy

I take my little books to Nili and I read to her. She is happy, I can read now. Mum bring all my long-ago story books to Nili, we look at the story books, my stories, about dinosaur, fire engine, car, butterfly. Nili help me to read my own stories.

I can copy the words on a page, I can read my story. I don't need pictures to read. All my stories got pictures.

From now – no more pictures. Just words.

CHAPTER 25

Claire

Joshy was being taught at his own pace, but Yasmine included him in as many lessons as possible, and surprisingly he was excelling in science. He seemed to have a really good visual understanding of three-dimensional space – he had always loved Lego and built very complicated rockets, spaceships, fire engines, but I thought that was just typical of kids' play, and now it seemed that in this area he was more competent than many other children in his class.

And increasingly, wonderfully, he was getting positive comments from Yasmine about his work at school. She had got her class involved in quite a complex construction project which involved building small model cars with wheels and axles, using only recycled materials. She gave the children used cotton reels, dowel rods, tape, twigs, and string, showed them the basic principles of axles, and let them get on with it. Joshy's car was fabulous. It had a steering mechanism which really worked, and he had painted it bright red. It was placed on the display table at the entrance to the school. He got a special mention at the next school assembly, and amazingly, a week later, a prize for the child who had made the most progress in reading in that school term.

* * *

In the meantime I was busy promoting P.A.L.S. Following my phone call to the local newspaper, I was interviewed by a lovely young woman who worked for the paper. She was fascinated, as she had never heard of S.L.I. We talked a while about the millions of children who are struggling to get a good education in South Africa, with its historic lack of schools and of good teacher training programmes.

The journalist herself was black and had, through the efforts of her own mother, got a university education and a well-paid job. Sadly she was one of a minority of black youth getting a really decent education. Many millions are still trapped in poverty, living lives of hunger and deprivation and attending schools which don't really meet their needs.

When we moved on to talk about S.L.I. and I gave her some examples of Joshy's difficulties, she initially asked me some tough questions. Maybe he is just a poor student? Not everyone is good at school. She was sympathetic and open-minded, but her job, she told me, was to play devil's advocate and to ask all the questions which her editor and the paper's readers would ask, so that she could answer them before they were asked.

I talked a lot, but felt that I had still not really explained S.L.I. well. So I asked her to accompany me on a visit to a local school for the deaf, which Nili had told me about, where only Sign Language is used. Nili had a speech therapy colleague who worked at this school and who was happy to show us around.

Some schools for the deaf promote oral talking as well as (or instead of) signing but this school had chosen to use mainly Sign. I had made it my business, before the visit, to learn a few signs, but the journalist was completely taken aback. She was a confident, articulate person who clearly could talk to anyone, anywhere, on any topic, and here she was placed in a situation where she couldn't talk to any of the children, didn't understand what they were saying, and just walked around, looking interestedly at everything but completely cut off from any real interaction.

It did give her an idea for future articles to be written – about other people with communication difficulties. She now wanted to research and write about people with autism, people with learning difficulties, with Down's syndrome, people who have had a stroke, and while I was thanking her for taking the time to listen to me, she was thanking me for giving her a good idea.

Nili

I ran a training session for the teachers at Joshy's school one late afternoon, about why children with S.L.I. might struggle with maths. Using examples from his maths book (without mentioning his name) I showed them that although children with S.L.I. might be quite able to understand and use numbers, to add or subtract or multiply, when it came to maths activities which involved understanding language, they would usually come a cropper. Word sums such as 'three boys went to the shop to buy sweets. They bought two sweets each. How many sweets did they buy?' were quite beyond children with S.L.I. due to their difficulty in understanding the language.

What does 'each' mean? Was does 'they' mean if you are not sure of the difference between he, she, and they? And how can you remember all those words, and then keep them in mind while working out the numbers? The language would be an impenetrable barrier and the child would be so busy trying to understand the words that by the time he got to the numbers, everyone else would have moved on to the next question.

Another area where maths is hard for children with S.L.I. is fractions, because the words 'above' and 'below' the line are confusing. 'Above' (assuming the child with S.L.I. has learned some words for place, which Joshy was still finding difficult) usually means 'higher' in three-dimensional space. How then does the child with S.L.I. understand that 'above the line' means something on a flat page?

How does a child with S.L.I understand that 'minus' and 'subtract' are the same as 'take away' when each new word he has to learn is a supreme memory task, and when the teacher sometimes uses one word and sometimes another, to say the same thing?

Not to mention 'positive' and 'negative' numbers. Joshy knew that his mum often said to Jenna, when she was in a sarcastic mood, "Don't be so negative". So how does a number feel negative? Joshy had also found it disconcerting when learning to tell the time. The hands of the clock didn't look like hands at all, they were long arrows and short arrows, so why were we talking about hands?

Claire had a good idea. She recorded the training session on video and we started looking for some funding to make copies of the video so that we could send it out to other schools. The sound quality was not great and I didn't like the way I looked on film, but we had our first P.A.L.S. product.

Joshy

Hello Granny, is Joshy here talking. I got lotta reading books, I got, wait, I counting.... I got seven books.

I got a prize at school for good reading! I made a car, it got wheels and string and I put a Lego man and he can drive the car. You want me to read you a book? I get a book and read you.

OK Mummy want to talk first, then I read to you.

I saw lotsa hadeda, all flying over the roof, what a noise!

Granny when you come to visit? I want you come to visit so I can read to you.

OK, bye! Oh yes, thank you for you send me the presents, the books, thank you Granny.

CHAPTER 26

Nili

Out of the blue, I was phoned by someone at the Education Department and asked if they could have a chat with me.

It was a job offer.

And it was something really tempting: to advise the department on how to support children with language delay in the classroom, in schools across the Western Cape.

For the department to realise that language delay was a big issue in schools was a big breakthrough. For them to be willing to fund a full-time post to deal with this was an even bigger deal. And it seemed like one of those serendipity moments, coming at a time when Claire was doing such wonderful advocacy work in promoting precisely this issue.

I was really tempted. Making people more aware of what can be done to help children with language delay is a topic close to my heart. And certainly, with all my years of experience in schools, I knew quite a lot about what teachers could be doing and how to help these children.

And yet this would involve leaving my actual hands-on work with children, those relationships which have been so precious to me over so many years.

I can remember so many of them, although I have no idea where most of them are now, and what they are doing. Sometimes I am lucky and meet one of 'my' children, or their parents, around town – one of the benefits of living in a smallish city – and catch up on what they are doing now they have left school.

But many of them remain in my mind at the age I last saw them, when they stopped coming to me for therapy. I think of their troubled selves at the start of therapy, of my all-too-frequent fears that I wouldn't know how to help this child develop language. I remember the times when therapy started to show results, the times when Vito and I celebrated a child's progress from incoherent sounds to a first word, or the first time a child made eye contact with me. I remember the sadness and the joys that I had shared with parents at each step of the way.

How could I give this up? It was a major part of my life, something which, no matter what was going on in my own life or with my family, gave me joyful, privileged, precious relationships with so many people. If I accepted the job offer, I would be advising teachers, writing policy statements, providing feedback to politicians, but not actually working with children like Joshy on a daily basis.

And yet on the other hand, how long could I go on being as energetic as I needed to be when working with young children? Many therapists of my age had already retired, and I have to admit I was tempted by the thought of a well-paid, high status job which would suit me well in my final years as a working person. I thought about it and talked endlessly to Vito, had a few meetings with people at the Education Department to find out more, and then asked for a little more time.

Claire

We made it into the national press! After the article in the local paper was printed, I got lots of calls from my friends who saw my picture and read the article. I have to say 'my' journalist had managed to say everything that I had been trying to explain, in a way which was much more coherent and concise than I had worded it. And then the story somehow got picked up by a journalist from a national newspaper and there I was, in the paper, looking rather glamorous.

The journalist had included my email address and I started getting emails: from worried parents, from teachers, from a head teacher working far away up in the north of the country, whose sister had sent him the article because she knew he was interested in language difficulties.

I had a lovely email from a woman who worked for a charity which trained volunteers to teach reading to kids in the townships, and she wanted to talk to me about those kids who simply were not making progress and who also seemed to have difficulties talking. The response was exciting and moving; I could see how we could have an impact on public awareness, on the lives of other kids, through the P.A.L.S. project.

P.A.L.S. was now keeping me very busy. After the initial excitement and glamour of interviews and photos, it became much more a matter of keeping the momentum going, and that involved lots of less exciting stuff, like arranging meetings and timetables for training sessions at schools, making sure that our letters had indeed arrived at the schools and had been read by the head teacher and not just by the receptionist who might have just filed them away for future reference. I was also contacted by someone in the Education Department who wondered whether we were doing enough to include the township schools, and Nili and I had a few discussions about how we could make the information accessible in different languages.

We also started to see that if P.A.L.S. was to grow, we might need to set it up as a formal charity, which meant having trustees, accounts, and a bigger organisation than I had wanted to be part of. We decided to let it run for a full year before we even thought about formalising things to that extent.

In the meantime Nili and I had visited three schools and given short talks to some of the teachers. It was proving quite difficult to timetable teacher training slots as these had usually been programmed at the start of the school year, so we were doing short talks tacked on to other people's training sessions, which was not ideal.

But with the combination of the talks, and the articles in the press, and an interview I did on talk radio, we felt we were really getting noticed. We started collecting a database of names of parents who were concerned, of teachers who were interested, and even some university lecturers who were studying early childhood development. I started sending out a weekly email, with letters from parents, and a language game in each email (Nili wrote that part), which could be made from recycled materials at home or in the classroom.

This was really important to us as we were now trying to reach township schools which did not have available funds to buy equipment or toys. We tried to provide a different type of game each week. One week it was vocabulary, one week understanding, one week grammar. Here is one of the games we sent out on our email.

***

VOCABULARY GAME: MATHS (SHAPES, QUANTITY)

TARGET WORDS:
Stage 1: CIRCLE, TRIANGLE, SQUARE
Stage 2: ALL OF, SOME OF.

EQUIPMENT:
Cardboard, scissors, crayons or paint. You can use old cereal boxes for the cardboard. A drawstring bag or box.

Cut out at least 10 small and 10 big triangles, squares and circles. You will then have 60 cards.

Paint or colour the cards so they are brightly coloured and attractive. Use lots of different colours; don't do all the same shapes in the same colour.

You can ask the children in your class to help you colour the cards.

HOW TO PLAY:

<u>To learn 'circle' 'square' and 'triangle'</u>: Put all the shapes in a bag. Each child takes a turn to take a shape from the bag and put it on the table.

The teacher names the shape. All the children can join in repeating the name of the shape. Once they are familiar with the shapes, let the children name them on their own. Repetition will help them learn the names.

Divide the shapes into groups: all the circles in one pile, all the triangles in another, all the squares in a third. Then each child has a turn to take one shape from any pile, and to say its size as well as its name: 'BIG CIRCLE' or 'SMALL SQUARE' etc.

<u>To learn 'all of' and 'some of'</u>: Give instructions to the children: J, can you pick up ALL OF the squares? M, give me SOME OF the circles. Initially you will have to give the instruction and do the action on your own, until the children understand what you mean by 'ALL OF' and 'SOME OF'. It may help if you explain that 'all of' means there are none left once they are all taken; 'some of' means that a few are left after some have been taken out.

Once the children have understood the game and the words, they can take turns to give instructions to each other.

REMEMBER:

ALWAYS SHOW THE CHILDREN WHAT YOU WANT THEM TO DO AND SAY BEFORE ASKING THEM TO DO IT.

GIVE THEM LOTS OF OPPORTUNITY FOR REPETITION!!

* * *

Joshy

My story. Nili write this story on paper and I copy it on my own page in my book. Nili now not writing in my book, it is my book, I am writing in my book.

Once upon a time, a big bird, Hadeda, came to visit the school. He fly over the school. That a nice school! I can see a playground, I can see swings and slides. Hadeda can see Joshy in the playground.

So Hadeda come down down down and lands in the playground. All the children stand in a circle. They looking at Hadeda. Joshy say, I know that bird, I know he name. He is Hadeda.

So Hadeda sit on Joshy's shoulder and they go in. They go in the class. Teacher says, who that? Who that bird? Joshy say, it is Hadeda. He come to learn maths. OK says teacher. This bird need a desk and a chair.

Joshy find a desk and chair for Hadeda. Hadeda can count, can do maths. Hadeda can read. He say, HAA-HAA-DE-DAA!!!!

Then he fly home to he house, he live in Kirstenbosch, he say bye Joshy! Bye! HAA-DE-BYE!

CHAPTER 27

Nili

A month or so later, I told Claire, in confidence, that I was considering taking the new job and leaving the school. I wanted to talk to her, outside of my office, about our continuing work on P.A.L.S., as well as to reassure her that Joshy would still be able to have speech therapy at the school, as they would be employing a new therapist if I did leave.

I suggested to Claire that we take Joshy on an outing where she and I could talk but where he could enjoy himself too. I decided that Boulders Beach, with its penguin reserve, would be a good place to go to, as it was away from the noise and bustle of town, and with Joshy's growing love of birds it would give him something to plan and to talk about.

The penguin reserve was originally started by a few local citizens who noticed that these charming birds, previously unseen on our coast, had started coming to Boulders Beach, and seemed to be nesting there. Boulders Beach is actually made up of a few connected beaches, with one reserved for penguins; the others are open to people. The people have to stick to their own beaches, but the penguins sometimes feel free to join us and to cross from one beach to another. I have, on one magical swim in one of the small ponds, actually swum next to a penguin.

It is a beautiful, peaceful place, where you can see nature conservation at its best: a safe haven for wildlife, in the middle of a residential seaside suburb.

Each beach is surrounded and sheltered by enormous grey granite boulders. Some of the boulders are the size of a house, other smaller ones the size of an elephant. You can walk between the boulders, stepping on the fine, soft white sand, and get to the sea.

The water rises very slowly with the incoming tide and flows gently around and between the boulders. It is so clear that you can still see the rippled whiteness of the sand through the water, even at high tide.

It is one of the places where I feel what Joshy must have felt in the drama tent. A space where people can be what they want to be, and where magical things can happen.

Claire

Nili invited Joshy and me on an outing. I had mixed feelings, because Nili had told me, in confidence as she had not yet made a final decision, that she might be leaving the school to take up a new job with the Education Department.

She assured me that the school would have a new therapist and that she would do a complete and thorough handover, and I knew that Joshy probably now had enough confidence to cope with a change like this. But childishly, I didn't want a new therapist. I wanted things to stay the same. I wanted Nili to be our therapist until Joshy no longer needed one.

Nili suggested that our meeting be held somewhere special, so that we could talk about P.A.L.S. but also as a kind of celebration of Joshy's hard work and his learning to read. She suggested we go to the penguin reserve at Boulders Beach, knowing how much he loves bird watching.

* * *

We bought our tickets and asked Joshy which of the two boardwalk tracks he wanted to take. Each one leads off in a different direction, winding through the reserve, and then curves around so that they end up opposite each other, above the penguins' beach, giving a good view without disturbing the nesting birds. He asked us to go one way and he wanted to take the other way, so we could wave to each other from the end of each track, across the small stretch of beach where only penguins are allowed to walk.

I knew it was perfectly safe as there is no way to get off the track once you are on it. Secure fencing, designed to keep people away from the penguin nest sites, also serves to keep small kids on the track so they can't wander off and get lost. So we set off on our different routes.

We got to the end quite quickly, chatting about P.A.L.S. and our plans, and I looked across to wave to Joshy.

No Joshy.

My heart skipped a beat. I looked behind me to see if he had perhaps followed us after all. No Joshy. We looked at each other for a split second and without saying a word turned back and ran along the boardwalk, past the tourists gawking at the penguins, along the winding track, up the steps, down the steps, past the penguins' shaded nesting sites and the toilet block.

We got to the ticket office, out of breath. I panted to the ticket seller, "My boy, my son, Joshy! I can't find him!" I could barely get the words out.

The woman smiled. "Do you mean the boy who saved the seal?"

She told us how a small boy, maybe five years old, had come running to the office, shouting quite loudly, "A seal is crying! Crying, on the rock!" And how the wardens had followed the boy, and found an injured seal, and captured the seal and taken him to the local vet, and that Joshy, our hero, was now sitting in the warden's office, eating an ice cream.

* * *

I had always dreamed about Joshy becoming more social as his language developed. I imagined how he would one day have lots of play dates and spend time with other boys. And though he had found a friend and seemed to enjoy spending time with Lukhanyo, he still seemed to prefer to do more solitary things: to be at home, to play with Lego or on his Play Station, or to go surfing. He would spend hours with his binoculars, staring at the trees outside in the hope of seeing a hadeda or guinea fowl. We suggested karate and tennis, and Joshy went a few times but didn't want to continue.

And now I saw my boy, sitting like a grown-up in the conservation office. He and the warden were actually having a kind of man-to-man discussion about their respective whale sightings of the season.

There was a look on Joshy's face which I had never seen before. It was a look of having found his home, an expression of confidence as well as a kind of nonchalant pride. This was my silent boy, who had heard the call of a seal, and by telling the wardens, by talking to the right people, had done something, when all the other tourists and visitors had heard nothing and done nothing.

EPILOGUE

Nili

This is a story about a boy learning to talk. It is also a story of gifts: a gift given to me in the form of my profession, which I love and have loved now for over twenty five years, and which has allowed me to change the lives of many children; the gift to Claire and Dave of their wonderful, interesting, sensitive boy; the gift of life which Joshy gave to the seal.

The gifts and the talking go on and on. Claire has hit her stride with her advocacy work for P.A.L.S. The Language Project is growing in ways we never anticipated. Recently, she was flown to Johannesburg by an education charity to give a talk on S.L.I. and how to support children like Joshy at school and at home.

But it is not only about talking. It is also a story about three people who learned to listen to each other, and about a boy who knew how to listen to a seal.

And though I have used a lot of words in telling the story of Joshy's therapy and his language, in a way that year was more about silence than about talk, more about listening than about speaking.

* * *

After the panic and drama of Joshy getting lost and found, we needed to sit down and recover. So we went to the café at the nearby Seaforth beach. Joshy had made a card for me. He had drawn two people, a woman and a small boy, and written, in his now much-improved handwriting,

"Thanks for you teaching me."

I looked at Joshy sitting confidently, tanned, relaxed, no frown lines between his eyes, scanning the horizon constantly for signs of life, for birds, for any sign or movement of whales in the bay. I watched this beautiful boy, this rider of waves, who had endured a daily struggle through the thickets and brambles of a windswept landscape, the jungle of the world of language, and who took the time and the care to listen to a seal.

Joshy

We went to Boulders Beach with Mum and Nili to see the penguins. Nili said she wants to go somewhere special, a special place. I said, the drama tent is a special place, and she said, that is true. It is a special place. And Boulders is also a special place.

We walked on the wooden track. The fence keeps people out so the penguins can have a nest. Sometimes people want to steal their eggs. So they got to have a fence.

It is a special place. The trees grow up and over your head so it is a green tunnel. We walk and see the penguins. Some live under the trees in the shade, and some make a nest on the beach. They turn their head all the way round to look at you. It smells like fish, 'cause penguins eat fish.

I go on one track, Mummy and Nili go the other way. I get to the end of the track and I can hear a funny sound.

I think it is a baby crying. I look at the rocks by the sea and hear the crying.

I can see a seal there, he is crying. So I go back on the track all the way back, up the steps, down the steps. I go past the trees, all the way. I go to the ticket office and tell the man the seal is crying on the rock.

He say come with me and I didn't want to, 'cause Mum says don't go with a strange man, but he is not a strange man, he sold us a ticket. So I went to the office and told the other man the seal is crying on the rock. So they said come with me.

We walk on the track, up the steps and down the steps, and in the green tunnel, and we get to the end and the seal is crying on the rock. So the men said, wait here, and they jump over the fence and walk on the beach, 'cause they allowed to, and give the seal a medicine and he go to sleep.

And they pick him up on a blanket and take him to the seal hospital to make him better.

Mum and Nili come running, where were you?

So I say, I hear the seal, the seal crying on a rock, I hear him so I answer him.

THE END

NOTES

Specific Language Impairment

The story of Joshy could be about any of the children with Specific Language Impairment with whom I have worked over the years.

For unknown reasons, children with S.L.I. develop language much later than other children, and sometimes continue to have very limited understanding and talking. They may struggle to express their ideas and their needs, and are often on the receiving end of teasing and bullying by peers, and do not have sufficient language to defend themselves.

Children with language disorders may be seen by adults or teachers as stupid, wilful, or rude, because they don't have the verbal or the non-verbal communication skills to follow instructions, to express their ideas, or to fit in with socially accepted rules of behaviour.

I have been privileged to see how children like Joshy can make remarkable progress in their language, as well as socially and academically, if they are provided with appropriate and timely speech and language therapy and teaching.

But at the same time I have been struck by how bewildering the diagnosis is for parents, and how little is known about S.L.I. by the public and even by many class teachers. Language disorder in children could be called a hidden disorder: unless you are trained to do so, you can't tell just by looking if a child has it. And yet S.L.I can have serious and long-term consequences for emotional development, academic achievement and social adjustment, not only in childhood but extending to adulthood as well.

When a child is first diagnosed with S.L.I., it is usually after the family has been worried about their child for a while, but are not sure what the problem actually is, and what can be done about it. For parents and families, making one's way through the thicket of referrals, diagnosis, long waiting lists for speech therapy, and the jargon often used by medical and para-medical professionals can be a very painful and bewildering experience.

According to research, S.L.I affects around seven percent of all children. This means that some 300,000 children in the UK alone are affected. It is said that there is one child with S.L.I. in every classroom. It is alarming that there is so little awareness in the public perception of a condition which affects so many children.

This book is a novel, but it is based on my 25 years' experience in working as a speech and language therapist with children like Joshy. The book aims, through telling the story of one such child, to demystify some of the issues which these children experience. It describes the impact of the disorder on the child's family, social life and schooling. It explains how speech therapy works and how families can get involved in their child's learning.

Only once there is sufficient awareness of the frequency of this disorder, and the devastating effect it can have on a child, will there be sufficient public demand for increased provision in the school and healthcare systems.

<u>Useful contacts</u>

I CAN: 8 Wakeley Street, London, EC1V 7QE, United Kingdom. Tel (U.K.) 0845 225 4071 or 020 7843 2510 http://www.ican.org.uk/

AFASIC: 1st Floor, 20 Bowling Green Lane, London EC1R 0BD, United Kingdom. Tel (U.K.) 0845 3 55 55 77 http://www.afasic.org.uk/help-for-your-child/afasic-helpline/

AFASIC have produced a book about advocacy. *The Parents Voice: Advocating for your Child.* www.afasicengland.org.uk

RALLI CAMPAIGN: Raise Awareness of Language Learning Impairments. http://www.youtube.com/user/RALLIcampaign

Wordworks. An education charity which does sterling work in the townships of Cape Town, South Africa. www.wordworks.org.za

Notes and references

These are a few of the writers who have informed my work with children with language disorder:

Danon-Boileau, Laurent. *The Silent Child: exploring the world of children who do not speak*. Oxford University Press, 2001.

Feuerstein, R. Rand, Y., Hoffman, M.B., & Miller, R. *Instrumental enrichment: An intervention program for cognitive modifiability*. Baltimore, MD. University Park Press, 1980, 2004.

Frankl, Victor. *The Will to Meaning*. Meridian, Penguin, 1988.

Maitland, Sara. *A Book of Silence*. Granta Publications, 2008.

Paley, Vivian Gussin. *Wally's Stories*. Harvard University Press, 1981.

Pellegrini, A. The relations between symbolic play and literate behaviour: a review and critique of the empirical literature. *Review of Educational Research 55*, 1985. pp 107-121

Phillips, Adam. *The Beast in the Nursery*. Faber and Faber, 1998. p 41, p 45

Swain, M. The Output Hypothesis and Beyond: Mediating acquisition through collaborative dialogue. In Lantolf, J.P. (Ed.) *Sociocultural Theory and Second*

Language Learning. Oxford: Oxford University Press, 2001. pp 97-114.

Wells, Gordon. *The Meaning Makers: Learning to Talk and Talking to Learn*. Multilingual Matters, 2nd Edition, 2009.

Winnicott, D. *Collected Papers: Through Paediatrics to Psychoanalysis*. London: Tavistock, 1958.

Notes on the text:

Chapter 6:
Counting the main words or 'information-carrying' words in a sentence or phrase is a way to assess a child's comprehension and auditory memory. It is also a way to assess a child's expressive language. The term refers to the words that carry meaning in a sentence, and not the redundant words. For example, in a sentence such as 'The boy is eating a banana' the words that carry meaning are 'boy', 'eating' and 'banana'. The redundant words are 'the', 'is' and 'a'. So this sentence has three information-carrying words.

Chapter 14:
In this book I have chosen to use capital letters to represent the speech sounds. This is not in accordance with the academically agreed-upon convention of using brackets such as /b/. I have done this to facilitate the publishing format of this book.

Many children, when young, will simplify the sounds G and K, and will pronounce them as D and T respectively.

This is called "fronting" because the sound is produced in the front of the mouth rather than at the back. If a child continues to do this after the age of about three and a half or four, it may be that the child will need the help of a speech therapist to correct these sounds.

Chapter 17:
From a phonetic point of view, that is, when we are saying the sounds aloud, K and C are identical. It is just a convention of spelling, of the written form of English, which requires one or the other.

Chapter 23:
Even though Joshy's story seems to have some very long sentences, they are not actually long sentences linguistically speaking, but rather a collection of short sentences joined together. I did not think it would be appropriate to be a stickler for theoretical linguistic accuracy when only a few months ago Joshy had been saying single words only. So we agreed that these were sentences with 28 and 25 words.